LAST SUMMER
IN
Algonac

LAST SUMMER
IN
Algonac

By Laurisa White Reyes

skyrocket
press

Skyrocket Press
28020 Newbird Drive
Santa Clarita, CA 91350
www.SkyrocketPress.com

Cover design by Blue Water Books
Interior design by Laurisa Reyes

ISBN: 978-1-947394-06-3

In memory of my grandma Dottie Ball,
my Aunt Larry Reid, and my mother Cyndi White,
the strongest and most remarkable women
I have ever known.

Dedicated to my children:
May you never take for granted those who came before you.

**A memory is a
photograph
taken by the heart.**

The Making of a Family Story

I FIRST LEARNED about my great grandfather's suicide in 1983. I was fifteen and interviewing my Grandma Dottie Ball for a school project. As she told me about her life, she mentioned, almost in passing, that her father had taken his own life when she was fourteen, and that had been the catalyst for her and her mother's move to California.

Later, in my mid-twenties, I developed a keen interest in family history and began researching my mother's family line. I was especially curious to know more about my great grandfather, Bertram Reid, and what circumstances had led to his death. Grandma knew very little. To her, it was a mystery.

I was fortunate to have a close relationship with Dottie's sister-in-law, Alice Larayne Reid, whom we all referred to as Aunt Larry. Larry was also a family history enthusiast and taught me much of what I know about genealogical research and record-keeping. On March 27, 1939, Larry had been the one to discover Bertram's body in his car in the garage, engine still running. Over many years, letters, and face-to-face interviews, I was able to piece together that tragic event, though no one really knows for sure why he killed himself. Some suspect he may have had cancer or some other illness. My grandmother remembered he'd had a sore on his leg that didn't seem to heal, so maybe he had Diabetes. But such suggestions are mere speculation. What I do know is that his death caused a massive shift in my grandmother's young life. Once she passed away in 2001, I was compelled to imagine how she might have felt at her father's passing, how she might have reacted, and how it might have affected her and the other members of her immediate family.

I spent many years simply thinking about things, asking questions, of Aunt Larry and of myself. I began trying to connect the dots through family photographs, census records, and details from the Reid family tree. I knew early on that I wanted to write a book about Bertram and Dottie, that theirs was a story that deserved to be told, to be remembered. The problem was I had no actual story. All I had were names, faces, dates, and locations. It took me two years just to decide *how* to tell this story that didn't exist. Should it be Larry's story? Bertram's story? Dottie's?

In 2017, I traveled with my daughter, Carissa, to Algonac, Michigan. Though at the time of Bertram's death in 1939 the family was living in Cleveland, he had immigrated from Canada with his parents and siblings in 1887 (he became a naturalized U.S. citizen in 1906) and settled in Algonac. The family built a home in Point Duchene near the Chris-Craft boat factory on the St. Clair River, and Algonac remained central to the Reid family's history for decades to come. In fact, Algonac had been integral to Dottie's childhood. Her grandfather was buried there, and eventually four additional members of her family would be buried in the same plot.

Carissa and I spent a wonderful week in Algonac. The St. Clair River is breathtaking, as is the abundance of green, which we're unused to in Southern California. I could see why the Reids loved it so much. Carissa and I spent a good deal of time exploring and doing research. We visited two local historical museums, tried to locate the original Reid home (without success), and hunted for the Reid cemetery plot (which was successful). Bertram is not buried there. He is buried in Cleveland at the Acacia Masonic Cemetery in Mayfield Heights, Ohio.

Following our trip, I spent the next few years outlining a plot for the story of my envisioned novel. First, with intensive research, I created a timeline from June 1938 to March 1939, framed with actual historical events and details from the era.

Next, I created characters from the family members I knew most about, their personalities based on the bits and pieces I'd gleaned from conversations and correspondence with Aunt Larry. I also created a few fictional characters to aid in the overall structure of the story. For example, the two African American housekeepers, Sadie and Marigold, are completely fictional. However, Grandma had told me on several occasions that her family had always had a "colored maid," even during the Depression. Her mother, Dorothy May, could not cook well. Grandma eventually learned to cook from her mother-in-law. So, that led me to believe that the Reid's maid did all the cooking throughout Dottie's life up to that point. It was common during that era for middle class white families to hire black help, so it was not a stretch to add one to Grandmother Reid's household as well.

Another made up character is Dottie's childhood friend, Walter. I needed some conflict in the story beyond the growing mystery and tension between Dottie and her father, and Dottie also needed someone to confide in. So, Walter, as well as her two school mates, Judy and Betty, were born. However, all the family members mentioned were real people, and I did my best to be as true to what I knew about them as I could.

Finally, I filled in the gaps between the historical facts and the characters with my imagination. I tried to create a believable story that could have happened. I imagined what Bertram, Dottie, Dorothy May and the others might have actually experienced, what events might have actually occurred. I brought in real events, such as

Algonac's first ever pickerel contest and boat parade for Independence Day, which really did occur in 1938, as well as Orson Welle's infamous radio play of *War of the Worlds*, a baseball game between the Cleveland Indians and the Detroit Tigers, and the release of Shirley Temple's *The Little Princess*.

In addition, I took liberties with some details to make the story "work" better. In the novel, they have a surprise visit from Clara Pratt, Dorothy May's mother. Clara (Noble) Pratt is one of my favorite people in my family history, and I really wanted her in this book. It made sense to include her since she was Bertram's mother-in-law and Dottie's Grandma, but I have no evidence that she ever visited Algonac.

Also, according to census records, Margaret Reid, Bertram's mother, and his sister, Florence, had already moved away from Algonac by 1938. In 1930, they were living with Arthur and Ethel Pohl in Detroit, and in 1940 they were in Dearborn with John & Hattie Witzig. I also chose to leave out the majority of Bertram's siblings—Ethel, Herbert, Harry, and Gordon—simply because I know nothing about them, and that would have been too many characters to keep track of. (My apologies to their descendants for not including them.)

The end result is that *Last Summer in Algonac* is my attempt to answer so many unanswerable questions and to give voice to a man who until now remained an enigma to our family. If others find it inaccurate or different from what they imagined, I apologize, but I've done my best with the limited information I had at my disposal.

I only learned a few years ago that not everyone in our family knew that Bertram had committed suicide. It simply wasn't discussed. In truth, until recently, with the prominent deaths of several celebrities such as Robin Williams, Anthony Bourdain, and Chris Cornell, suicide has been a taboo subject in our society. Especially in the early part of the 20th century, I suspect suicide would have caused a family shame and resentment. While I have no records of the Reid's finances at the time, the fact that Dottie and Dorothy relocated to California and that Dorothy May Reid worked as a "child nurse" in a private home (1940 U.S. Census), it seems evident that Bertram's death caused not only emotional trauma but financial upheaval for the family. His decision to end his life abruptly changed the trajectory of theirs.

In 1939, it was unlikely that my grandma or her family (or Bertram) had access to mental health care or therapy, which is almost a given today. They faced the most horrific of losses and had no choice but to deal with it as best they could. I am certain Grandma, as well as her mother, sister, and brother, were forever altered by Bertram's death, but they handled it surprisingly well, from what I can tell. I am tempted to chalk it up to resilience, but I think their emotional and mental survival was born of necessity.

Honestly, after all the time I've spent on this story, I've come to see my grandmother and great grandmother in a new light. They were incredibly strong women, and their strength has been passed down through the succeeding generations. So many of my siblings and cousins, and our children, have faced tremendous adversity of all kinds and so far have powered through it in admirable ways. I like to think we all take after Dottie Ball, Dorothy May Reid, and Clara Pratt—that we are intricately linked. I believe they would be proud of how we've all gotten on with our lives, that we've *chosen* to get on with our lives. In that sense, *Last Summer in Algonac* is Bertram's story, but it is also Dottie and Dorothy's story, that when faced with unimaginable hardship, they took hold of each other and pressed on.

Sincerely,

Laurisa White Reyes

Part One:
Algonac – Summer 1938

June 6, 1938

Dear Walter,

Winter lasted forever, don't you think? We were still getting snow in the middle of March! I'm sure it was worse for you than it's been here in Cleveland. I don't mind the snow so much as I do the cold wind. I never will get used to it. My sister Alberta lived in California for a time, and she says it's nothing but sunshine all year round. Can you imagine?

Fortunately, the bad weather is behind us, and summer is well on its way. I'm so looking forward to seeing you again. I'll hold you to your promise to take me out in your family's new boat.

I can always tell when it's time to visit Algonac by the way Father whistles when he mows the lawn on Sunday afternoons. He just seems a bit more chipper this time of year, and who can blame him? Michigan is still home to him, I suppose, and in a way I can't explain, it is for me too, even though I didn't actually grow up there. There's just something magical about Algonac and the St. Clair. Of course, you already know that since it really is home to you.

My friends Betty and Judy say I'll miss all the fun while I'm gone and promised to keep in touch. They've got grand plans for summer, but I don't mind. I'll make my own fun with you in Algonac.

See you soon.

Sincerely,

Dottie Reid

Come to think of it, I haven't heard Father whistling yet...

Chapter One

IT'S STRANGE THAT even after all the years—decades—that have passed since Father's death, I know as little about him now as I did then. You'd think a daughter would know her parent, and for a time I thought I did.

Bertram Wallace Reid was a man of average height, but strong and lean. He had the well-toned shape of a swimmer, and he did love to swim, or at least that's what Alberta told me, though I saw little evidence of it myself. That was partly due, perhaps, because by the time I was born in 1925, Father was already forty-four years of age and past his prime. But from what my older siblings tell me, in his younger days he spent many a summer afternoon doing laps along the banks of the St. Clair or splashing in the shallows with Alberta and Charles when they were children.

I have a photo of Father's sister, Hattie, standing at the bow of a rowboat dressed in a dark wool bathing costume, her arms held out from her sides as though poised to dive into the water. I don't know who took the image, maybe it was Father or one of his other many brothers or sisters, but I have to believe that Father had often stood on that very prow as a young man, smiling, laughing, jumping into the water. Swimming.

That last summer in Algonac, there was little water play for

Father, who was now fifty-seven. Alberta, who had married less than two years earlier and had recently given birth to her first child, had opted to stay in Cleveland. She and Charles had been my grandest playmates while I was growing up, but now they both had new adult lives and families of their own. Even Charles, who was eleven years my senior (Alberta fourteen years) would prove too occupied with his wife Alice and their baby to venture into any games with me. I supposed Father might have played that role with me when I was young, but I was thirteen now, practically a woman, and neither he nor I dared suggest something so childish as to jump into the river for a splash—except for that one last wonderful afternoon.

Looking back, I wish that I had done it every day—that I had taken his hand and walked with him along the bank under the trees, or sat in the grass and taken off our shoes, letting our feet dangle in the chilled, meandering water. I wish that I had had the courage to ask him more about that old rowboat, whether he had ever taken it all the way across the river to Ontario, Canada, where he and his family had come from originally. I would have liked to have been in that boat with him rowing, his muscles taut under his shirt, his sleeves rolled to the elbow.

We wouldn't have talked much. Father was a man of few words. But I would have listened to the ripples of the St. Clair lapping against the boat, the gentle cut of the oars through the water, the calls of birds overhead. It would have been enough just to be with him, to see his face turned to the sun, the light glinting off his spectacles, and to have seen traces of a smile on his lips.

1939, the year Father died, was a big year for America. It was the year the World's Fair opened in New York, and the first shots of World War II were fired in Poland. *The Wizard of Oz* premiered at Groman's Chinese Theater in Hollywood, California, and Lou Gehrig gave his final speech in Yankee Stadium. Theodore Roosevelt had his head dedicated on Mt. Rushmore, and John Steinbeck published *The Grapes of Wrath*. All in all, it was a monumental year, one I would have liked to have shared with my father. He did live long enough for Amelia Earhart to be officially declared dead after she disappeared over the Atlantic nearly two years earlier, but otherwise he missed the rest of it.

No child should have to mourn a parent. And if she does, at least things about it should be clear. Unanswered questions that plague one for the rest of one's life shouldn't be part of the picture.

Death is normally simple, isn't it? Someone has a heart attack, or dies in a car accident, or passes away in his sleep of old age. Everyone expects to die sometime, and they wonder how it will happen and why. And when it does, as sad as it is for those left behind, the wonder is laid to rest.

Most of the time.

1939 was a blur. I'd prefer to forget it, quite frankly. But 1938 was worth remembering, especially that summer we spent in Algonac with Grandmother Reid and the family. As long as I could remember, we'd spent every summer on the banks of the St. Clair. As it turned out, it would be my final summer in Algonac. Our last summer together. Of course, I didn't know it at the time, and I'm glad. If I could have seen seven months into the future, if I had known then how the world as I knew it would all come crashing down, it would have spoiled everything.

Summer officially began in the middle of June, the day after school let out. Charles, Alice, and baby Gary were over at the house trying to hurry Mother and I along, though I was the one dawdling, if truth be told.

"Knickers, get down from there!"

In my room, I wrapped my arms around our fat calico cat, lifted his limp body from the bed, and set him on the floor. After rubbing against my leg and receiving his customary scratch behind the ears, Knickers slipped from the room and scampered away down the hall.

3

My bed was neatly made, the coverlet smooth and proper, but I tugged at a corner just the same. I wanted it to be just as perfect when I returned home in August. Standing back, I gave it a final nod of approval then turned to the open carpet bag on the floor.

"Ain't you packed yet?" asked Sadie, wiping her hands on her frilly white apron. "Young Mr. Reid's already brought the car 'round and got most the luggage in the trunk, all but yours," she added with a critical glare.

Sadie had been with our family for as long as I could remember. Even longer. When the Depression hit a few years after I was born, Sadie had stayed on even when Father couldn't afford to pay her a full salary. He had made it up to her, though, when better times came along. No matter what people said about keeping it business with the coloreds, as far as I was concerned, Sadie was part of the family.

"I don't see why you're not coming with us." I had repeated this same complaint several times already. Sadie opened the top drawer of my bureau and pulled out my favorite green nightgown. She carefully placed it in the bag on top of the rest of my things, then buckled the strap shut.

"Your grandmother has her own help," said Sadie. "I'd just be in the way. 'Sides. I'm needed here. Who else is gonna see after Knickers while you're gone?"

I felt dejected. Though Sadie had never gone to Algonac with us before, I didn't see why she couldn't come now, but when I'd suggested it to Mother the night before, she had peered at me like I'd gone off my rocker and then went back to arranging the pantry without so much as a yes or no.

"You all packed now?" asked Sadie.

I picked up the carpet bag. It felt heavy, but then I suddenly remembered what was missing. I dropped the bag, which elicited an eyeroll from Sadie, and snatched my copy of *Elsie Dinsmore* from the nightstand.

4

"I thought you already read that," said Sadie.

"Twice," I replied. "But I've started it again." I opened the bag and placed it carefully on top, and then refastened the strap. "Now I'm packed."

"'Bout time. I'll just git this out to the car."

As Sadie lifted the bag, a car horn blared from outside. I hurried to the window and drew back the drapes. Our big black Lincoln was parked out front, its trunk open wide. Charles sat at the wheel drumming his fingers while Mother stood at the curb, her hands cupped over her mouth.

"Dorothy!" Mother hollered. "Dorothy Ann Reid, do you expect me to wait here all day?"

Charles honked the horn again.

"You'd better get a move on," said Sadie, "or your mama will tan your hide!"

I followed Sadie down the hall and out the front door. Sadie set the bag in the trunk and shut it with a bang while I dutifully slid into the back seat of the car beside Alice. I reached for four-week-old Gary who was squirming unhappily in his mother's arms. "Let me take him for a few minutes," I said.

Alice handed him over. As soon as Gary was in my arms he calmed down and promptly fell asleep.

"You're a godsend," said Alice with a relieved sigh. "You've got the magic touch. I was afraid he'd be fussy the whole ride, and you know how your mother is about noise."

Alice and Charles had just celebrated their second wedding anniversary in May. I had liked her from the start. A trim, cheerful girl just ten years my senior, Alice felt more like a schoolgirl chum than a grown-up. I looked at Gary's sleeping face. With his blonde wisps of hair and rosy cheeks, he looked so much like Alice.

Outside the car, Mother gave last minute orders to Sadie. "Draw the drapes each night, but not before six or the sun will damage them.

5

And be sure to dust the lamp shades every Saturday."

"Don't I always?" said Sadie, trying not to laugh, and winking at me through the open car window. "And don't you worry 'bout that cat, Mrs. Reid. You know how Knickers loves me."

"That's just fine," said Mother. "We will be arriving home toward the end of July."

"More'n a month by the river. Sound like paradise to me."

"It isn't paradise," replied Mother, opening the car door and sliding into the front seat beside Charles. "It's Algonac."

Mother rolled up her window and smoothed her dress over her lap. "All right, everyone. It's time to go fetch your father."

Chapter Two

CHARLES RELEASED THE Lincoln's parking brake, and the car rolled forward. In just a few hours we would arrive at the Reid Family home where we'd spent every summer since before I was born. But first, we had to stop at the Union Club.

Charles guided the Lincoln against the curb in front of the four-story edifice. With its pale granite blocks and monolithic scalloped columns, it had always reminded me of the ancient architectures of Rome and Greece.

"Hurry now," Mother instructed me. "Tell the man not to dawdle."

I carefully handed Gary back to Alice before getting out of the car and racing up the front steps. Jimmy, the doorman dressed in his neat doubled-buttoned jacket and gleaming brass buttons, greeted me with a tip of his cap.

"G'day, Ms. Dorothy. How's that sister of yours doing these days? Haven't seen her in a while."

I always stopped to chat with Jimmy when I came for Father, but today I didn't have much time, with Mother waiting impatiently in the car. Still, I didn't want to appear rude.

"It's been more than two years now since she and Harold Oberg married," I told Jimmy, glancing back at the car. "Alberta had a baby last year. A boy. Didn't Father tell you?"

Jimmy laughed. "Well, now that you mention it, I believe he did. Will she be going with you to Algonac this year?"

"I'm afraid not," I said. "The baby's caught a cold, but she might come for a visit later."

Jimmy smiled as proudly as if Alberta had been his own daughter. "You tell her I said hello. Wasn't that long ago she was the one running up these steps. You have a good day now, y'hear?"

He pushed open the heavy door, and I darted inside.

The Union Club of Cleveland was and still is an iconic hallmark of city tradition. Established in 1872, it was founded as a place where men could enjoy reading and conversation about the issues of the day, though the current location wasn't purchased until 1901. Through the years, its membership has boasted several United States Presidents, including Ulysses S. Grant and William McKinley, as well as many business tycoons, inventors, and countless other respected members of Cleveland society. Though intended for men, the club has included a Ladies' Lounge since 1882.

The building was designed by Charles F. Schweinfurth, who had also designed many of the mansions on Millionaire's Row. The interior was breathtaking, with wide mahogany pillars, sculpted inset ceilings, and a grand marble staircase fit for royalty.

But I didn't have time to admire all that now. I had a mission to fulfill.

I hurried down the hall past the lounge, ignoring the disapproving glances from the men dressed in dark suits and encased in clouds of cigar smoke, though my flurry didn't seem to distract them from their serious conversations.

Finally, I reached Father's shop, boxes of cigarettes and cigars neatly displayed in the glass case.

"When did the club start letting in little girls?" Father asked, peering at me over the rim of his spectacles. Father wasn't a particularly tall man, but he had broad shoulders and large hands, and his face normally displayed a perpetual smile and a hint of mischief. He wore his graying hair slicked straight back and would never be caught without a white handkerchief in his blazer pocket.

"You'd better beware," Father added, a glint of humor in his eye, "you keep coming in here, one of these fine gentlemen just might propose marriage."

"Daddy!" I said, rolling my eyes, then I leaned over the counter and placed a kiss on his cheek. "Do you know what day it is?"

"Why, I don't really know. I thought it was Saturday."

"Yesterday was the last day of school, and you know what that means."

Father fished in his pocket and retrieved his favorite lighter, the silver one Mother gave him the Christmas before I was born. "It means you've finally finished middle school," he said. "Hurrah for you. Now, you're a high schooler, but how can that be? My little Polka Dot isn't more than five years old."

"I'm thirteen, Daddy."

Father laughed and slipped a cigarette between his lips. "Of course you are. So, if school's out…"

"Today we're leaving for Algonac! Mother says not to dawdle."

"Did she now? Well, then, maybe I should spend a few minutes taking inventory. Several boxes of Monteros arrived today. Not my preference, but some of the men—"

"Daddy, we really have to go. The car is waiting outside. And little Gary might wake up if we wait too long. And we've still got hours to go."

Coming around to the front of the counter, he pulled down the wood-slatted casing and locked it with a key. Then he dropped the key into his pocket, eliciting a crinkling sound. Father frowned as he withdrew a folded slip of yellow paper. He didn't open or read it, but I could tell from the expression on his face that he knew what the letter contained and didn't like it.

"What's that?" I asked.

Father didn't reply at first, and I wondered if he'd heard me. But then he crumpled the paper into his fist. "Nothing important," he said.

He snapped open his lighter and held the spark to the paper. It quickly ignited in a bloom of orange flame, which he then used to light his cigarette. Then he tossed the burning ball into a metal waste can.

Father stared at the can for a moment, his thoughts drifting. He took a long draw from his cigarette and pushed the smoke out through his nostrils. As he did so, he gave a little cough.

"Dry throat," he said. Then he took my hand and gave it a gentle squeeze. Mine felt so small in his, but safe too. "Let's not keep Mother waiting any longer, shall we?"

I slipped my arm through his, and together we headed for the entrance. I must admit I felt rather dignified strolling along beside him. To me, he was the grandest gentleman in the place. As Jimmy opened the door for us, Father gave me a brief smile, but it wasn't his usual smile. There was something different about it, something missing.

I should have known then that something had changed with Father, but that moment of realization was just a fleeting thought soon forgotten by the thrill of reaching Algonac and the adventurous summer waiting for us there. That moment wouldn't come back to me until long after Father was gone.

Jimmy followed us to the Lincoln and let me in the back seat where Charles now sat beside Alice, while Father climbed into the driver's seat.

"Morning, Chic," he said to Charles. "Morning, Larry," he said to Alice. And a moment later we were off.

Chapter Three

THE FOUR-HOUR DRIVE to Algonac from Cleveland felt longer than I had remembered. Maybe it was because baby Gary only slept for the first hour and then spent the rest of drive fussing, which caused a perpetual frown to crease Mother's face. Luckily, since she was in the front seat with Father, I didn't have to look at her except when she occasionally cast disapproving glances at Alice over her shoulder.

Alice, Charles, and I traded Gary back and forth through most of the trip. Father was never flustered by Gary's noise. In fact, at one point Father let Charles drive while Father doted on the baby, cradling him expertly in his arms and singing him lullabies. While watching him play grandpa to Gary, I imagined Father doing the same for me when I was small. I'm sure he must have, though I don't remember.

Finally, our Lincoln turned into Point Duchene, at the east end of Algonac, and rolled along the bank of the St. Clair past the Chris-Craft boat factory. The moment the river was in sight, I rolled down my window to get a better look. I like to think that the color blue came from the St. Clair, the deepest, richest shade of it I've ever seen. Even later, when Mother and I migrated west to California and I stood for the first time on the shore of the Pacific Ocean, the cobalt currents of the St. Clair reigned supreme in my mind.

For hundreds of years, this area had been the home of Indian tribes, like the Algonquins, Ottowas, Kickapoos, and Chippewas. The Indians named the river Otsi-Keta-Sippi. The first European to travel these waters was Robert Cavelier de La Salle in 1679 who named the river after the Catholic patron Saint Clare of Assisi. In the 1700s, French fur traders navigated the river, and by the end of the 18th century, the French and English had begun to settle here. An Indian agent by the name of Henry R. Schoolcraft christened the town Algonac, "Ac" meaning land or earth, and "Algon" taken from the Indian tribe Algonquin. By 1843, the name had stuck.

More than forty miles long, the St. Clair flows south from Lake Huron to Lake St. Clair and was the ideal location for a boat factory. While the elongated wooden building on the riverbank partially blocked our street view of the river, I didn't mind. I could always see it from the window of Grandmother's attic.

Father parked the car in front of the Reid's two-story Victorian-style family home. The structure, painted a calm shade of blue, was built by Grandfather Reid, Father, and Uncles Herbert and Gordon in 1920, and had been the family home ever since. After Grandfather's death in 1922, it had been primarily inhabited by Grandmother Reid and her aging housekeeper, Marigold.

As I climbed out of the car, Grandmother pushed open the screen door to greet us. She wasn't a tall woman, but she was regal-looking with white hair pulled back from her face in a loose bun, her hands clasped in front of her just below her ample bosom. She wore a full-length frock and a white cooking apron. Her stern expression observed all of us like a monarch inspecting her subjugates, but I had learned early in life that Grandmother's bark was worse than her bite.

"The trip went well, I hope?" Grandmother Reid said as Father pulled the cases from the car trunk.

"Fine, Mother. Just fine." He carried two, one in each hand, up the porch steps, then planted a kiss on Grandmother's cheek.

"Your rooms are waiting," she said. "Marigold's turned down the beds for you. Supper's at five, as usual."

Charles took another case from the trunk and led Alice with the baby up to the porch. "Grandmother, you remember Alice."

Following Father's example, Alice kissed Grandmother's cheek as well. The older woman gave a clipped smile. "And this is little Gary?" she asked, her tough exterior melting just a little. "Let me take him."

She reached for the just waking infant and cradled him in the crook of her elbow like an expert, which she was. Mother to seven children herself and grandmother to eight, Grandmother Reid knew all about babies. She cooed at the tiny boy and gently bobbed him, her other guests all but forgotten.

"Hello Grandmother," I said stepping up to the porch, my carpet bag in hand.

Grandmother glanced up from the baby as if she'd not realized anyone else was present. But when she saw me, her eyes warmed, and her first real smile appeared.

"Dorothy Ann." Grandmother always used my first and middle names, running the sounds together as if the two were one long squashed-together word. "My, you've grown these past months. Before long, you'll be taller than your mother."

She said this with a glance at Mother who was the last to reach the porch. Mother dutifully kissed Grandmother's cheek, but there was no warmth in it.

"Mrs. Reid," said Mother by way of greeting, then moved on into the house. When my parents first met, the Reids had not approved of the match at first. But Bertram loved Dorothy May and married her anyway. The two women had remained aloof ever since.

I followed Mother into the house along with Grandmother, still carrying Gary. "I've got the attic all fixed up for you, Dorothy Ann,"

13

said Grandmother. "I know how you like the view from up there."

How right she was. I took the stairs two at a time, flying past the second floor to the short flight of steps leading to the attic, a small room with a wooden floor, a steeply gabled roof, and a single window. No one else in the family liked the attic, claiming it was too small and stuffy, but ever since I could remember, this had been my favorite spot in the entire house.

I laid my bag on the freshly made bed and moved to the circle of beveled glass overlooking the street like a ship's porthole. Below in the drive was the Lincoln, and beyond that the street and Chris-Craft's factory. But beyond that was the river, its wide sapphire expanse reaching from bank to bank, its water lazily meandering by as if it had nowhere to go and all the time in the world to get there. Just seeing the St. Clair filled me with excitement.

"You jus' get here, Ms. Dorothy?" a lovely familiar voice said from the doorway. I spun and dashed into Marigold's arms. Marigold had been Grandmother's maid for longer than I'd been alive, maybe even longer than Father had been alive. She was as old as Grandmother herself, plump and soft as a goose down pillow, her sparkling eyes set above a perpetual smile.

"Just now," I said, relishing Marigold's embrace. "And Chic has come too, with the baby."

Marigold's smile grew wider. "Oh my! Is that so? I remember changing your brother's diapers when he was nothing but a sprout. Now I guess I'll be changing another generation of Reids." She laughed a contented, genuine laugh that made me feel more at home than I ever did in Cleveland.

"I'm so glad to be here," I said.

Marigold laid a hand on my cheek. "I'm glad, too. More'n you know. House gets awful quiet during the year now most everyone's moved on to the city."

"Oh, but Father says Aunt Hat visits often. And Auntie Florence is still here in Algonac, isn't she?"

"Yes, course she is. She looks in on your grandmother every day. Sometimes I think Florence stays a spinster on purpose, jus' so she can stay free to care for her Ma. She's a good daughter, that one is, even if she is jus' a little bit unconventional."

Marigold gave my cheek a gentle pat before turning to leave. "I got lunch ready in the kitchen when you're unpacked. Come on down and grab yo'self a sandwich."

"Cucumber?"

"Course! I know it's your favorite. But I got some chicken salad too. And fruit salad. And lemonade."

My mouth began to water. No one made better cucumber sandwiches and lemonade than Marigold.

"And when you've had your fill," Marigold's expression turned slightly mischievous, "I happen to know of a certain someone who's been waitin' all spring for you. And he wouldn't be too happy if you postpone sayin' hello before too long."

Walter! Just the suggestion of my old friend made my heart feel about to burst with excitement. The only child of Grandmother's neighbors, the Smith's, Walter and I had known each other our entire lives and were each other's best summertime playmates.

"I'll run over right after lunch," I promised.

Marigold smiled again and then headed back downstairs. I quickly emptied my carpet bag and set the carefully folded socks and underclothes into the dresser drawers and then hung my dresses and slacks in the wardrobe, but before following Marigold, I returned to the window to catch another glimpse of the river.

Father was outside. He stood facing the direction of the water, his back to the house and the car. He raised a cigarette to his lips and drew in a long, casual breath. He held the smoke in his lungs a few moments before letting it out through his nostrils, like he did when he was thinking deeply, which he seemed to be doing now.

15

He'd grown up in this town, at least since his family had immigrated here from Canada in 1887, so he knew it better than anyone. I loved summers here, where Father always seemed more relaxed than he ever did at home, as if he'd somehow left the serious side of himself behind in Cleveland and arrived in Algonac a few worries lighter. He stood straighter here, smiled more, frowned less. It was his natural habitat. That was a term I had learned in science that year.

Algonac was where Father belonged.

But today I noticed something different about him. It wasn't anything I could decipher easily, just a feeling I got that I couldn't put into words. Was it that his shoulders seemed to slump forward just a bit, or that he let the ashes burn on the tip of his cigarette longer than usual, as if his thoughts had drifted?

"Dorothy Ann!" Grandmother called up the stairs. "Come down for lunch now, y'hear? We're all waiting for you."

Someone must have delivered a similar message to Father because he turned then and nodded toward the porch. I watched as he took one last drag on his cigarette and then threw it on the ground and crushed it beneath the toe of his shoe. But it was when he lifted his face, pausing as if sensing my eyes on him and then glancing up to the window, that I noticed it. Just for a split moment. That mask of concern when our eyes connected, and then it was instantly gone. He smiled up at me and shifted his head just a bit to the left, summoning me down from my tower.

Chapter Four

BY THE TIME I made it to the kitchen, Father was already seated at the table with a glass of lemonade in his hand. The alcove that served as Grandmother's dining area was sardined with Reids, each feasting on Marigold's sandwiches. Even Gary, now nestled in Charles' arms, was enjoying a warm bottle of milk.

Marigold handed me a napkin. "Help yo'self, Missy, before they all gone."

I snatched two cucumber sandwiches off the platter. Just as I remembered from all my previous summers there, the bread, probably freshly baked that morning, was soft and sweet, the cucumbers crisp and cold. I loved the taste of cream cheese and dill, picked out of Grandmother's box garden in the kitchen window.

"Aunt Hat called over," said Charles, finishing off a triangle of chicken salad sandwich. "She and John got in from Dearborn yesterday and are staying at the Inn. There's a race tomorrow morning. John's betting on McGregor's new Streamliner."

Mother dabbed the corners of her mouth with her ring finger. "As long as we are all unpacked and get ourselves a solid night's sleep, might be a nice way to spend the day."

Marigold beamed. "I could whip up some fried chicken and

potato salad for lunch. We could take a basket."

The bottle nipple popped out of Gary's mouth, and he instantly protested. Alice reached over and maneuvered the nipple back into place.

"What do you think, Dad?" asked Charles. "Shall we go to the race tomorrow?"

Father finished off his lemonade. Marigold was quick to refill it from the crystal pitcher. He drank another half-glassful before responding. Father never rushed into anything, especially conversation. He was a thoughtful type, cautious with his words.

"I suppose," he said finally, setting his glass on the table with deliberate care, "a boat race would be the right way to start our summer holiday." His lips pulled into a grin, and then he gave me a wink.

Suddenly, the kitchen was filled with excited conversation: Marigold and Grandmother discussing meal plans for tomorrow, Charles and Father debating the capabilities of the latest Chris-Craft models, and Mother giving advice to Alice about the right way to burp Gary, as if Alice didn't already know.

This seemed the perfect time to slip away and see Walter. I snatched another two sandwiches from the nearly empty platter and darted for the front door.

"I'll be back soon," I said, but no one seemed to notice.

We'd left Cleveland just after noon. Now it was nearly five o'clock, though the sun was still high and bright as ever, casting diamonds of light across the river. I loved how summer days seemed to stretch on forever, and I loved filling those days with every adventure I could think of.

Walter Smith had lived two doors down from Grandmother's my entire thirteen years. Like Grandmother Reid, the Smiths were year-rounders, braving the fierce winters of Algonac as well as its calm summers. Walter and I had first been introduced as babies and had remained loyal summer friends ever since.

I climbed the steps to the Smith's porch and rapped on their screen door. It opened a few moments later, and the face of Bethie, their maid, appeared. Bethie, who was just in her twenties and had only married the previous year, scoured me with her eyes.

"Hmm-hmm," she said with exaggerated disapproval. "Why if it isn't Miss Dottie Reid herself, finally seen fit to bestow her presence on these steps after a long, long, long absence from the palace."

I tried not to laugh, but I couldn't keep it in. A giggle escaped my lips, and Bethie broke into a warm, wide smile.

"It's about time I see you," she added, her joking gone. "Come here and give me some sugar."

I let Bethie envelope me in a strong embrace. "It's good to see you too, Bethie," I said. "It's been a long year."

"Sho has." Bethie stepped back. "But at least you have something of a normal life out there in Cleveland. Here, we been hibernatin' all year. And poor Mr. Walter, he been bored outa his mind!"

"Is he here?"

Bethie shook her head. "He's down by the canal. Why don't you see if you can't find him? And tell him to come home for supper, while you're at it."

"I will! Thanks, Bethie."

I practically leapt off the Smith's porch, momentarily forgetting that I was in a dress and was supposed to be acting "feminine," as Mother often reminded me. But right now, I didn't care about any of that.

I found Walter just where I expected, sitting on the bank of the canal just around the corner from his house. Algonac was criss-crossed with narrow canals connecting homes throughout the city to the river. Walter's back was to the street, his spine arched forward, his knees bent nearly to his chest. His pants were rolled up past his ankles, and a fishing rod extended in front of him, the line trailing to

19

the right downstream. From where I stood, I could see his mussed brown hair clipped short at the neck and around the ears but longish on top. I'd recognize the shape of him anywhere.

I watched him for a minute, bobbing the rod a little, trying to attract a fish. I knew from experience that he would sit there for hours until he'd collected enough fish for Bethie to prepare for dinner that night. There'd been plenty of times in the past when I had sat right alongside him.

I was tempted to sneak up on him, give him a start that would set us both laughing. But before I could approach him, Walter straightened suddenly. He paused as if listening or sensing something in the air, then he turned.

When his blue eyes connected with mine, something inside of me jumped, but I immediately brushed aside the feeling. This was just Walter, after all.

Walter's mouth spread into an easy grin. "I thought I heard someone prowling around over there," he said.

"I wasn't prowling," I replied, closing the distance between us. As I neared, I noted how changed he looked from the previous summer. Then, he'd been a little chubby, though I'd never have told him so. In the year that had passed, Walter, who was fourteen now, had slimmed down. The muscles in his forearms were defined, the hands gripping the rod firm, like a man's hands.

Walter patted the space on the grass beside him.

"My dress," I said, instantly regretting my choice of clothes. Why hadn't I changed into something less girlish?

Walter tipped his head back and squinted one eye at me. "That never stopped you before. Your mother used to wag that finger of hers when you'd come home all mussed up after fishing with me."

"That happened once, when I was nine."

"Even so…"

I folded my skirt around my knees and tried to sit as daintily as I

20

could, which was virtually impossible. In the end, I just let myself plop onto the grass.

Walter chuckled and shook his head. "What's happened to you? You get all girly on me?"

I glared at him and saw that his face, too, had narrowed and that there was a hint of future whiskers above his lip.

"What if I have gone girly? I'm nearly fourteen now, you know. Mother says I've got to grow up sometime."

Walter lifted his rod and reeled in the line. Then he pulled back his arm and cast it out again.

"Any luck so far?" I asked.

"A few." Walter nodded to a basket sitting on the grass beside him, its lid down but unlatched. "Enough for supper. Been here since just after lunch. Was just about to pack up when you showed up."

I leaned back, bracing my hands behind me in the cool grass. "You knew I was coming today, didn't you? I didn't surprise you at all."

Walter gave the line a couple of quick tugs, then he laughed like he'd been caught sneaking cookies. "Marigold told Bethie last night you were coming." He cast me a sideways glance. "Plus, I seen your Pa's car pull up 'bout an hour ago."

I sat up and faced Walter. "Then why in heavens didn't you come say hello?"

Walter shrugged and started reeling in his line again. "You know how I am around all those people." And I did. Walter shied away from crowds. He didn't even like being in school where he clammed up and was labeled shy as a child. He'd often told me I was the only one he really felt comfortable with, which made the years between summers long for him. "Besides," continued Walter, "I knew you'd eventually come looking for me."

"Walter Smith!" I gave him a playful smack on his shoulder which triggered laughter from both of us.

Walter finished pulling in his line, then he stood and propped the rod against his shoulder like a rifle. "I gotta get these to Bethie," he said. "Why don't you come say hello to Ma. She'd love to see you."

I realized then that there was no ladylike way to get up from the grass, not with a dress on. I considered my situation and determined I'd need to roll to my knees to get purchase, as the slope was too steep to rely solely on my feet to get myself up. In the past, I wouldn't have cared. Like I said, this was just Walter. But for some reason, today felt different. I didn't want to make an unladylike impression. As if sensing my quandary, Walter held out his hand.

I took it and with a firm but gentle pull, I was on my feet and admittedly a little out of breath. It wasn't until we had both stepped up to the level street that I realized that Walter had changed in more ways than one.

"Since when did you get so tall, Walter Smith?" I said, noting that for the first time ever, I had to look up to meet his gaze. I'd always been an inch or two taller than him, but now he was a good two inches taller than me.

Walter laughed again and snatched up the fish basket before striding down the street. He took several steps before turning back to look at me.

"Are you comin' or aren't you?"

I thought Algonac was just the way I'd left it ten months earlier, but now I wasn't so sure. Seemed more had changed than I'd realized.

"I'm coming," I said, then hurried to catch up.

Chapter Five

THE NEXT MORNING, I awoke to bright sunlight streaming in through the attic window. I glanced at the clock on my bedside table. Nearly eight! How could I have slept in so late?

I quickly dressed and made my way downstairs where Marigold was already washing dishes in the sink, her blouse sleeves rolled up to her elbows.

"Saved some breakfast for you," she told me after I'd given her a quick hug.

"Why didn't you call me down?"

"What, and disturb your first morning on holiday?" Marigold nodded toward the dining table. "Eggs are still hot."

I slid into a chair and breathed in the delicious scent of sausage, scrambled eggs, and buttered toast.

"The house is so quiet," I said between bites. "Where is everyone?"

Marigold dried a plate with a towel and set it in the cupboard. "Miss Alice is still in the bedroom with the baby. Your grandmother, Mr. Bertram, Ms. Dorothy, and Mr. Charles went to Sunday service and then headed over to your Aunt Florence's to say hello. They'll be back in time for today's races. In the meantime, how 'bout you lend me a hand with the fried chicken."

Marigold and I spent the next couple of hours cutting chicken, dipping the pieces in buttermilk batter, and carefully lowering them into a kettle of hot oil. I loved watching the breading turn deep golden brown and crispy. Then we ladled each piece onto a towel to sop up the excess oil. The smell of it made my mouth water.

Alice joined us after a while, baby Gary happy in his bassinet. She and I finished the chicken while Marigold started the potato salad. We were just packing everything up when Grandmother and the rest of my family arrived home.

The races were set to start at noon, said Grandmother, which meant with any luck the boats would be ready by one. So, we took our time loading up the Lincoln and Grandmothers' Buick and driving into town. We really didn't have far to go and could have walked, but with all the food and Grandmother and little Gary, Father suggested driving would be best.

We parked just a mile down the road near the public park. Most of the big races took place on the lake about sixteen miles away. But today, the Chris-Craft factory was sponsoring a local competition to kick-off summer.

We climbed out of the cars and headed for the riverbank, Marigold with one basket on her arm and Charles with the other. As everyone marched along, I lingered behind with Father.

It was a beautiful day to be at the river, a cloudless sky overhead reflecting the brilliant blue of the water. Father strolled casually along, one hand in his pocket, the other moving a cigarette lazily in and out of his mouth between breaths. While the others hurried on, anxious to reach their destination, Father seemed in no hurry at all.

"We'll fall behind," I said, hoping to urge him on. "You don't want to miss the first race, do you?"

Father took a drag from his cigarette. "They never start on time, you know."

As he exhaled, smoke circled his head. I thought it made him look like a spirit or a ghost. "Why don't you run up ahead?" he continued. "Give Larry some company. God help us all if your mother starts in on her again."

I laughed, catching the hint of a smile on his lips. Father was a man of few words normally, reserved and restrained, particularly around Mother who was quick to criticize should he offer an opinion with which she disagreed. But when he and I were alone, Father often had plenty to say.

"You see there," he said, pointing his cigarette across the St. Clair to the far bank of Walpole Island. "Canada. Sometimes it feels like I could just swim home again."

Of course, I knew it was Canada, that the river formed a boundary between the two nations. I'd been to Walpole by ferry many times, though unlike boating to Harsens Island, which was U.S. owned, I had to have my passport with me.

"When I was a boy, my father brought us here so he could find work." Father's steps slowed even more, and I matched my pace to his. "I always intended to go back, you see. Left a lot of good people behind, friends, family. But eventually I met your mother, got married, had Chic and Bertie."

Chic and Bertie were Father's nicknames for Charles and Alberta.

He took another pull from his cigarette, then he tossed the stub to the ground and crushed it underfoot. "Then you came along," he added, cutting me a smile. "Though you took your sweet time about it. I was well into my forties when you were born, did you know that? Your mother was thirty-eight. I recall your sister, who had just started high school at the time, her response when Mother told her the news. She was aghast."

Father chuckled at the memory. "But once you arrived, she fell in love with you. We all did, you know. Me most of all."

"So, you never went back?"

"Oh, I have a few times for visits, but Cleveland became my home, you see. I suppose I stopped wanting to go back."

"Why is that, Daddy?"

"Because here became more important to me than there. Does that make sense?"

I wasn't exactly sure it did, but I nodded anyway. Then I slipped my hand into his. I didn't care that I wasn't a little girl anymore. When I was with Father, I felt like nothing else in the world mattered except the two of us.

We all arrived at the picnic area beside the St. Clair. Dozens of Algonac's residents had already gathered there to await the start of the race, and hundreds more lined the bank for a mile or more. I tried to spot familiar faces among the crowd when a hand shot up above the sea of heads, waving frantically.

"Yoo hoo! Charles! Alice! Over here!"

Aunt Hat waved them over to where her husband, John, and their children John Jr. and Ruth, who were eleven and ten years respectively, reclined on an expansive patchwork quilt. Hattie Witzig was one of Father's three living sisters. She and her family owned a summer home in Algonac not far from Grandmother's.

John, in his late thirties with a generous girth and thinning hair, sat with his legs splayed out in front of him, stockinged feet wriggling in the breeze. He leaned back on his elbows and peered up at us from beneath the brim of his straw boater.

Father held out a hand, which John shook vigorously. "Hope you brought some cash," he said. "I aim to win at least ten dollars off you today, Bert, my boy."

"Fine. That's fine," said Father. "But perhaps I can interest you in a box of White Owls instead."

"Cigars?" Uncle John grinned. "You're on!"

Harriet Reid Witzig, Aunt Hat for short, was taller than most women and thin as an Aspen. She nearly matched her husband's height and stood out like a signpost amid the crowd of race goers. Dressed in a calf-length light blue frock with laced sleeves to her elbows, Hat greeted each of us with an enthusiastic embrace. "Oh, Alice! Gary is just adorable! Couldn't be sweeter!" she said, pinching the baby's cheeks.

When she came to me, Hat took me by the shoulders and smiled. "My oh my. What a beauty you've turned out to be," she said. "I'm sure you'll be turning plenty of heads this summer."

"Now, Harriet," scolded Grandmother, "enough of that now. Marigold made her fried chicken and a platter of deviled eggs."

"Why, that's just perfect!" said Hat, bestowing a one-armed hug on Marigold. "That'll go just fine with the watermelon slices and salmon salad we brought, won't it, John?"

John patted the spot beside him on the quilt, and Father sat down cross-legged beside him while Mother and Charles laid out a blanket of their own beside Hat's. Hat nestled next to Alice and amused herself with baby Gary while Charles joined the other men. Marigold set about unpacking dishes for the picnic.

"Let me help," I offered, reaching into the basket for the bowl of potato salad.

"Don't you be snitching any of that 'fore your grandmother gets her share, now. Y'hear?" But Marigold just laughed when I snatched a piece of watermelon and bit into it. Sweet red juice dribbled down my chin, but it tasted so good I didn't care. Marigold quickly grabbed a cloth napkin and handed it over. "Good?" she asked.

"Mmm-hmmm," I answered, my mouth full.

"Be sure you finish that up quick 'fore one of Missus Harriet's kids come asking for some. Those two could finish off that whole plate 'fore the rest of us gets a bite."

On the river, several boats puttered by, their captains waving at the crowds. They were sleek, some sixteen feet long, others twenty or twenty-four, rich mahogany buffed to a high shine. I loved the varied styles of the Chris-Craft and Gar Wood designs, manufactured with the utmost care right here in Algonac at the factory just across the street from Grandmother's home. Boating had been part of my life ever since I could remember.

John pointed to one of the boats cutting a sharp trough in the water as it sped by, its driver majestically standing at the wheel. "That there is the new Streamliner," he said, pointing out the passing boat. "Twenty-two feet long with three cockpits. Engine is aft. I hear it's got plenty of speed."

Unlike other boats that came to a decisive point at the front, the Streamliner's bow had no distinctive edges but came to a sleek, elegant curve that reminded me of an ancient oil lamp. Its wood was a deep, lush red. Plenty of room for passengers, and a little blue flag flying from its stern.

"I'm putting my money on the Streamliner," said John. "Her owner Bill McGregor's been boasting about her for weeks now. At least that's what I hear."

Father watched as the new star of the river conducted a wide turn and then came to a slow drift not far offshore. "Seems you've picked yourself a winner," he said, nodding his approval. "But for the fun of it, I'll place my bet on that nineteen-foot Runabout over there. She's a beaut."

Grandmother, overhearing the men's conversation, tsked disapprovingly. "This is just a local exhibition for men to show off their new boats. The real racing's in July."

Marigold started piling food on the plates and handing them out, first to Grandmother, then to Father and John, and then the others. Only once all the grown-ups had begun eating did Marigold give me the go ahead to help myself, which I did.

"Mmmm, Marigold," I said after sinking my teeth into a crispy drumstick. "No one makes fried chicken better than you do."

Marigold beamed. "I know it. Best in the county, so some folks tell me."

"Absolutely! I hope there's enough for seconds."

"Course there is! Here." Marigold set a thick juicy breast on my plate. "But you better take yours now 'fore those men come for more." Then she added in a giggling whisper, "I saved the biggest piece for you."

As I started in on the breast, Alice sat down beside me.

"Where's the baby?" I asked.

"With his daddy." She nodded toward the men where Charles held Gary in one arm and gestured toward the boats with the other, deep in conversation with Father and Uncle John.

Alice reached for a slice of watermelon. "I think summer is my favorite season," she said. "I could eat nothing but watermelon all day."

"Me too, Miss Alice," said Marigold. "What a fine day for it."

"It certainly is. The sky couldn't be bluer, I'm sure. What do you two say about walking into town after the races?"

Marigold smiled but shook her head. "I'll have to take all these dishes back to the house and get them washed up for supper."

Alice perked up. "Oh, then let us help you. We're good dish washers, aren't we, Dottie? We do it all the time at home."

"I couldn't," Marigold protested. "Missus Reid wouldn't have it."

Alice grinned mischievously. "She doesn't have to know. I'll ask her to take Gary on a walk in his pram. And we'll wash like the devil!"

In the river, boat engines revved. The race officiator stood on the shore, shouting into his megaphone. But the words were too garbled for me to understand.

"I think they're ready to start," I said, pointing at the two boats floating near the starting line. Other boats were gathered behind them, waiting for their turn.

A shot rang out, and the engines roared to life as both boats sped down river kicking up massive whitewater wakes behind them. They jetted forward, speeding along the surface of the St. Clair. I had heard Father say once that the speed record set in 1932 by Gar Wood's Miss America X was 125.4 miles per hour, though I'd since learned that just the previous year Malcolm Campbell reached 126 miles per hour. But to Father, Gar Wood was the only racer worth his salt. He built his boats in Algonac, and that, said Father, earned his loyalty.

The races continued as Marigold, Alice, and I packed up the soiled dishes and leftover food. Hat lent a hand, urging the men to eat up the rest of the chicken or let it go to waste. Father, Charles, and Uncle John obliged her, and soon all the food was gone, making the basket lighter for the journey home.

Seeing the other women getting ready to leave, Grandmother stood and smoothed down her skirt. "I'll come with you. The men can bring the cars around later."

"Oh, no, Mrs. Reid," said Marigold with exaggerated concern. "You just finished off a big meal. Why don't you stay a while and watch the races? Let all that food settle 'fore you head home."

Hat agreed with Marigold wholeheartedly. "That's right, stay a while longer, Mother. I don't want to be the only lady with all these men."

I cast Alice a glance as a reminder. "Oh, Mother Reid," Alice said as if suddenly thinking of it. "Would you mind terribly if I leave the baby with you? I've a bit of a headache coming on, and I'd like to lay down for a bit. You could even take him for a walk later in his pram. I'll leave his bottle."

Grandmother, of course, agreed. And on her insistence, Charles handed Gary over.

So, Grandmother Reid stayed behind while Marigold, Alice, and I walked home.

Along the way, I kept a lookout for Walter. He'd said he'd find me at the races, but he hadn't shown up. I'd feel bad if he came for me after I'd gone. But halfway home, there he was, jogging up the lane toward the river. He spotted me and waved. I waved back.

When he reached us, he was out of breath. "Leaving already?" he asked, hands on his knees, glinting up at me.

"We've got to wash these dishes," I said.

"Well, I'll come help."

"But I thought you wanted to watch the races. Father and Chic are still there. You could sit with them. They wouldn't mind."

Walter straightened and looked toward the crowd behind them on the riverbank, considering my offer. But then he shook his head. "Naw," he said. "I came to see you, not any boats."

He reached for the basket on Marigold's arm, and she gave it up with a girly grin.

"Now, come on, Miss Dorothy. If this boy wants to wash dishes, I say let him wash dishes. Give me a chance to start in on supper."

"What are you having tonight, Marigold?" asked Walter.

"Ham and black-eyed peas and collard greens, just like my granny used to make 'em."

"Sounds delicious. Am I invited?" Walter smiled, his eyes twinkling. Marigold had always had a soft spot for Walter. She giggled and told him she'd be offended if he didn't eat supper with the Reid's that night.

Walter thanked her and trudged on ahead with Alice and the basket.

Marigold held back. "Ain't the same boy you said goodbye to last summer, is he?"

I tried not to show my shock at Marigold's comment, but I had to admit that she was right.

Chapter Six

"YOU DIDN'T WRITE."

Walter had his hands buried deep in a basin of suds. With a rag, he rinsed one of Grandmother's picnic dishes clean and handed it to me to dry.

"I did write," I told him. "Well, at least that one letter a few weeks ago. I'm sorry."

"You promised you would."

I set the dish on the stack of those we'd already washed, the clink of the china resonating through the kitchen.

"I guess school caught up with me. It's been a busy year."

"Sure. Here too."

"Besides," I continued, wiping the last plate dry and adding it to the others, "I don't recall getting any letters from you either."

Walter glanced at me with a sheepish grin. "No, I guess you didn't."

I handed him my damp towel, and he dried his hands. Then he lifted the stack of dishes and set them in the cupboard. Alice and Marigold were at the dining table planning meals for the week. Walter and I moved to the porch, where a warm breeze blew, and sat down on the bench swing. I noted that some of the white paint had cracked since last year and was peeling off in narrow chips.

"Looks like this old swing could use a new coat of paint," I said, scratching my nail across a flaky patch. "Winter takes its toll on things around here, doesn't it?"

Walter nodded. "Good thing you weren't here to see it this year. Worst storm I've ever seen. Drifts so high they nearly reached the top of the utility poles."

I laughed a little, trying to imagine such a sight, but Walter was earnest.

"No kidding," he said. "Snow fell for more'n two days solid. My father told me they measured thirty inches deep. For three whole days, no one went anywhere. Not by car or train, until the roads got plowed, which was quite a feat, let me tell you. I heard a few people died even, like that lumberjack who froze to death in his truck. I'm telling you, it was something."

Father had read me some of the news reports in the paper about the bad weather up north. He was concerned about Grandmother, but being as he was four hours away in Cleveland, he had to rely on Aunt Florence and Marigold to take care of her. Though he did spend more time than usual puffing on his cigarettes in the front yard that month.

"Well, it's all gone now," I told Walter, gesturing to the leafy canopy draped over Grandmother's porch roof. "Not a sign of winter left."

"Except for the damage it caused, like the battered paint on this swing. I think I have a can of whitewash in my garage. I'll touch it up for you tomorrow if you like."

"If Grandmother likes," I corrected. "But I'm sure she would appreciate it."

We sat quietly for a while, enjoying the rhythm of the swing and soft swish of the leaves rustling in the breeze. I thought of the river flowing lazily past and longed to sit on the bank with my feet dangling in it. But before I could suggest it to Walter, Grandmother's Buick rumbled around the corner and parked in front of the house. Out climbed Father, Mother, and Grandmother with Gary asleep in her arms, the latter fanning herself vigorously with a paper fan. The Charles followed a minute later driving the Lincoln.

"I'll never get used to these humid summers," Grandmother said, taking Father's hand to climb the steps to the porch. "The heat, the humidity, the bugs."

"No one's forcing you to live here," said Father with a laugh.

"Well," Grandmother replied, "your father, God rest his soul, brought me here, brought us all here. He's buried here, so I figure I'm obligated to stay."

Mother joined Father and Grandmother on the porch. "We've offered many a time for you to live with us in Cleveland," she said. "And so has Hattie."

Charles took the baby and headed inside to find Alice. Grandmother lowered herself into a cushioned chair and kept fanning herself. "The city? Why, I'd shrivel in all that hubub and noise! Imagine me, trotting down Millionaire's Row rubbing elbows with the likes of John Rockefeller."

"Rockefeller died two years ago," said Father, lighting a cigarette. "Besides, Forest Hills was divided up years ago by his son, sold off to various organizations. Part of it's a high school now."

"A school? How befitting," said Grandmother.

Mother turned her attention to me. "Have the dishes been washed and put away, Dorothy?"

"Yes, Mother."

"And has Marigold started preparing supper?"

"Yes, Mother."

Father, sat down on the end of the porch swing and spread his arm across the back of it. "So," he said, "how are you, Walter?"

"I'm fine, Mr. Reid. Thank you," Walter replied.

"Why didn't I see you at the boat races?"

"Well," said Walter, "I thought I'd help out Dottie and your daughter-in-law instead."

"Oh," said Father. "You mean Larry."

Walter looked at me with confusion. "Larry?"

I laughed. "Daddy's nickname for Alice. Her middle name is Larayne, so he calls her Larry."

"I see," Walter said, though I could tell he didn't quite.

"And how is your mother?" Mother, clearly impatient with the conversation, directed it to a topic more along her interest.

"Doing just fine," Walter replied respectfully, "and looking forward to visiting with you, I'm certain."

Mother considered this a moment. "I'll drop by this evening after supper. Please let her know, will you? I'm going in to see what I can do to help Marigold along with supper."

Once Mother had stepped inside, Walter glanced at me and smiled. "I hope you don't mind my saying so, but your mother intimidates me just a bit."

"Just a bit?" said Grandmother, her fan pausing. "If truth be told, she's the reason I won't move to Cleveland."

"Now, Mother," said Father without any real malice. "You know Dorothy May is fond of you. She's sincere."

"I don't doubt it, Bertram. But I've enough starch in my laundry, thank you very much!"

Grandmother grinned at her own joke. I'd always liked Grandmother Reid. She could be pretty starchy herself when she wanted to be, but overall, she was a tolerant woman with a bit of humor always lurking just below the surface. I thought Father took after her.

He slid a hand into his pocket and drew out his cigarette case. "John and I are going fishing in the morning," he said.

Grandmother began fanning herself again. "I'll let Marigold know. Baked walleye with dilled potatoes would make a fine supper for tomorrow."

Fishing was one of Father's simple pleasures. He didn't do it often while at home, but come summer, he and Uncle John were sure to make time for it. And hunting too. They usually kept Marigold plenty busy preparing their catches.

"What about Chic?" I asked.

"Can't make it," said Father. "He promised to take your mother into to town to do some shopping."

Fishing was a man's world. At least that's what Mother had always told me. Most of my life I'd envied Charles each time he'd head off with Father and come back with a basket of walleye or perch, or a string of ducks or small game. I'd been keenly aware of their camaraderie, the looks of pride cast between them as if there was some secret only the two of them shared.

"I'll go with you," I said before I even knew what I was doing.

Grandmother's mouth fairly dropped wide open. "You can't go fishing," she guffawed.

"Why not?"

"It isn't done."

"I can learn, can't I, Daddy?" He'd taught me to use his hunting rifle shooting bottles in the back yard, much to Mother's chagrin, I might add. I was sure he'd be willing to show me how to cast a line as well.

He looked from me to Walter, as if my offer to accompany him was an automatic invitation to Walter as well.

"I've got other plans," Walter said quickly. "But I'm sure Dot would bring home the finest trophy."

Good old Walter.

"Well? Can I come?" I persisted. Deep down, I had no real expectation of being included. I'd never gone fishing before. Why should now be any different. But as Father's gaze drifted from me toward the river, I saw something in his countenance I'd noticed

36

more of in the past couple of days. A sort of deep, wandering thought. Father had always been contemplative, for example taking his time before answering a question or rephrasing something someone said to make sure he understood them correctly. But this was different. The way he looked off into the distance, it was as if he was considering something not physically there, something deep in his mind.

He appeared that way now.

"I'd like you to come along, Polka Dot," he said, taking a puff of his cigarette.

Grandmother fanned even faster. "Dorothy May may have something to say about that."

Father laid a hand on Grandmother's shoulder and smiled at her. "Don't you worry about that." Then to me he added, "Up at five. And wear a hat."

Then Father took a deep breath, opened the door, and stepped inside the house. I couldn't help but wonder if facing Mother felt akin to going to battle. Either way, I felt elated. I couldn't believe my good fortune! I, Dorothy Ann Reid, was going walleye fishing for the very first time!

Chapter Seven

AUNT FLORENCE SWOOPED in Sunday evening to greet us all. I say swooped because that is exactly how her visit felt. Most of us were in the front room listening to the radio broadcast when the door flew open and in she came, out of breath and fanning herself like a hummingbird.

Grandmother was the only one not to flinch at her sudden and unexpected arrival, used, I supposed, to Florence's comings and goings.

"Hidey ho, everyone!" Florence said quickly shutting the door behind her. She was carrying a canvas bag stuffed to overflowing, which she set on the floor. "Sorry I didn't come sooner, but I've just come from the market and bought up all the day's unsold corn and carrots and parships and what not. Can't pass up a bargain like that! Marigold!" Florence hollered through the door to the kitchen. Marigold appeared in an instant, as unperturbed by Florence as Grandmother.

"Mind taking these and putting them in the root bin? There's a girl, much appreciated. I hope you can make good use of them. I did swipe a few for myself, hope you don't mind."

Florence giggled. Her voice was high and rich and full of life. Of course, I'd known Florence my entire life and was thrilled to see her.

I leapt from my chair and threw my arms around her.

"Goodness!" she said. "You've grown, Polka Dot. By next summer you'll be as tall as me."

Florence was tall, the tallest of her sisters and a little taller than Father even. And she was long and lanky in limb with strong hands and an endless supply of energy. But what I loved most about Florence was her perpetual smile and her flashing dark eyes that seemed always to be thinking two steps ahead.

Father greeted his younger sister with a kiss on the cheek, while Alice and Charles did the same. Mother too gave her a brief embrace. Mother liked Florence, though I think she tired Mother out.

"Is that the news?" Florence asked, indicating the radio. "Well, I've got news for you too. You know, I'm on the Rotary committee, and we've just finalized the plans for the 4th of July. You'll see it all in the paper tomorrow. We'll have the races, of course, but we'll begin with a parade! A boat parade commencing upriver, and midway here we'll have a ceremony honoring three of our Civil War veterans. Won't that be jolly? Then the parade will end right here in Algonac! Then that night we're going to have a fireworks show over the water. What say you to that?"

Charles and Father and Alice gave a hearty cheer.

"Sounds like the perfect way to celebrate our independence," said Charles. "As long as they host that pie eating contest like last year, I'll be happy."

"My word!" said Florence with a hearty laugh, "Pie AND watermelon! In fact, I'm hoping Marigold might donate one of her famous huckleberry pies?"

From the kitchen, Marigold's voice called out. "Shore I will. And a peach pie to boot!"

Florence settled into the empty spot on the sofa that Charles had made for her by scooting closer to Alice. Grandmother had already turned off the radio.

"We could really use some volunteers to help put up decorations, run booths, that sort of thing." Florence was simply exuberant. She'd prided herself on being part of the Rotary for the past ten years and had aspirations to one day be president. "But right now, I need help passing out these mimeographs door to door so everyone can plan ahead."

Alice seemed to catch Florence's enthusiasm and was the first to volunteer. "Of course, I'll help. I'll just put Gary in his pram and do it while I take him for a morning walk."

Of course, I couldn't let Alice go it alone. "I'll go too," I said, but then I remembered my plans with Father. "Oh, wait. I won't be here tomorrow. Father's taking me fishing."

Florence raised her eyebrows and gave a little nod of impressed approval. "That's all right," she said. "It can wait a day or two, as long as we get them out this week."

I brightened again. "We'll go Tuesday then. Alice? Is that all right?"

"Perfect," said Alice.

"And maybe Walter can come too. And I'm certain we can all help with anything else you need."

Father, Mother, and Charles also agreed to help. Florence was ecstatic.

"Thank you all," she said, clasping her hands together. "I'll bring the leaflets round tomorrow evening. And we'll be hanging patriotic displays on the posts around town."

With that, Grandmother announced it was time for her to turn in, which generally meant the evening was over. But as most everyone turned in for the night, Father stayed behind to chat with his sister. I wasn't ready to go to bed, so I asked Father if he wouldn't mind my listening to the radio a little while longer.

"Go ahead," he said, "just turn the volume down. I don't want your grandmother charging in here wondering what all the racket is."

"Why don't you and I go out on the porch?" suggested Florence. "It's cooled so nicely."

I turned the dial on the radio and tuned into a station playing "Our Gal Sunday," my favorite broadcast. Father and Florence stepped outside, closing the screen door behind them so I could just hear their voices over the radio. All was quiet at first except for the familiar *click* of Father's lighter followed by him coughing just a little.

"Are you all right, Bert?" Florence asked in a low voice.

"Just a dry throat," Father answered. "It's this weather."

"What about...you know. Have you heard back from the doctor?"

Curious now, I stepped to the door to peer through the screen. The smoke from Father's cigarette curled around his head like a halo.

"Yes, but he said there's nothing to worry about."

"Pain in the chest seems worth the worry to me," said Florence.

"I thought so too, but he said my heart is fine. Strong. Probably just indigestion."

There was a moment of silence, which for Aunt Florence was unusual. I thought back to the slip of paper Father had burned at the club yesterday. Had that been the doctor's response? And why hadn't I known he'd seen a doctor?

"You are going to tell Dorothy May." Florence's voice was so quiet now I could barely hear her. But I saw Father shake his head and take another drag from his smoke.

"Why cause concern over nothing?" he replied.

He and Florence then moved away from the door, probably to sit on the bench swing. I soon heard the slow creak of the swing's chains. I'm sure they continued talking, but I heard nothing more. On one hand, I wondered what had happened to Father to prompt him to see a doctor. He'd obviously been concerned enough to tell his sister about it, but not enough to tell me or Mother. And the doctor had examined him and found nothing wrong, so as Father said, there was nothing to worry about.

The program ended, and I switched off the radio. I still wasn't sleepy, but I climbed the stairs to the attic anyway. I opened the window and let the cool evening breeze roll in from off the river. I turned off the light and lay on my bed, watching the crescent moon outside. Like Father and his cigarette smoke, the moon was haloed with thin wisps of clouds that partially obscured it, as though it was intentionally concealing itself, a child's game of hide and seek.

I see you, I silently mouthed to the moon before drifting off to sleep.

Sunday, June 19, 1938

Dearest Judy,

Sorry for the delay in writing, but I've been having so much fun here in Algonac that I just couldn't find a moment before today. How is Betty? I hear she's been busy sitting for her aunt. She sounds a bit disappointed but seems glad for the extra dollar a week. I hope the two of you will have a chance to spend it soon.

Thanks for the photograph of you at Shaker Lakes. As you know, Grandmother's house is near the St. Clair River, and I can see it from my bedroom window. I never tire of gazing at it, but I like swimming in it even more.

You asked about Walter. He says hello and that if you and your family ever visit Algonac, he will show you around town. As I write this, I have the most exciting news. Father has agreed to take me fishing. I've never been, though Father is an experienced fisherman and every summer brings home plenty of walleye for our suppers. Mother isn't too pleased. She thinks it's unladylike, but I'll soon be fourteen, and Grandmother says I'm old enough to make up my own mind. I'll let you know how I do. I was surprised when Father invited me along. He'd never allowed it before. Maybe it's the weather, but Father seems more pensive than usual, like his mind is somewhere else half the time. Maybe no one else has noticed, but I have.

I'll say goodnight as we're leaving before sun-up, and I want to make sure I'm good and rested. I promise to write again soon.

Sincerely,

Dottie

Chapter Eight

THERE'S SOMETHING MAGICAL about a river. Real rivers. The kind you find in the eastern part of the country. After moving to California in 1939, I only got to see those sorts of rivers on the rare trips I took back to Ohio and Michigan.

The Los Angeles River isn't what I'd call a river at all. It's just a long cement trough built to contain the rain waters that flow down from the mountains during a storm, and storms are rare things in Los Angeles. That river is dry most of the time.

No, the sort of river I'm talking about is the kind where you can stand on its bank and the other side seems so far away it's like another world, as if the blue expanse in between is a universe all its own. The water is always moving, the current languidly traveling downstream toward a lake or the sea. And it calls to you. Like a siren. The always present music of the water luring you into its depths. And once you get there, you can get lost in it.

I've been to the ocean hundreds of times over the decades I've lived on the West Coast, and I love the roar of its waves slamming against the shore, the calls of seagulls clamoring for food. But nothing can quite compare to the gentle purr of the St. Clair.

Sometimes, even now, I can hear it in my dreams. Calling to me.

I woke up before dawn that Monday morning and was dressed in slacks and one of father's old flannels before he'd even had his coffee. I was almost too excited to eat the eggs and bacon Marigold had prepared for us, but Father insisted I'd need my energy.

"You got a hat?" he asked as I finished off my orange juice.

I showed him the canvas bucket hat I'd borrowed from Grandmother, and he nodded his approval. Charles let me borrow his rod, and once we'd grabbed Marigold's egg salad sandwiches and fruit salad, we headed out to the dock to wait for Uncle John.

The sun was just peeking over the horizon when John motored up in his boat, a 1937 Sportsman. His pride and joy. "Climb aboard!"

"So, Dorothy May said yes, did she?" he asked, taking my hand to help me in.

Father stepped in behind me. "She eventually came round," he said with a sly grin. I hadn't been privy to the conversation of the previous night. I thought it best to let Father handle it. All I cared about was that I got to go fishing. I didn't much care how things arrived at that result. No matter what reservations Mother might have had, she would change her mind once I brought home enough walleye for supper.

The boat's motor hummed as we made our way downstream toward Lake St. Clair. It didn't take long before we'd arrived at the flats at the southeastern end of Harsen's Island and made our way into deeper water.

The St. Clair flows south for more than forty miles, connecting Lake Huron to Lake St. Clair, a vast 430 square mile fresh water lake, though it is diminutive compared to Lake Eerie to its south, which is nearly 10,000 square miles. But the St. Clair was plenty of space for us.

Uncle John turned off the motor and threw the anchor overboard. The lake wasn't deep, just eleven feet at its deepest. The men immediately got to work setting their hooks and filling the fish box with water from the lake. Once their rods were ready, Father turned to me.

"Now Polka Dot, let's see if you can set your bait."

I'd seen Father and Charles tie worms onto their hooks dozens of times. And last summer Walter had offered to let me try, but the business seemed too disgusting for me. But this time I was determined to prove Father hadn't wasted his time bringing me along.

"John, you've got those night crawlers?"

John retrieved a metal bucket from behind his seat. "Right here," he said.

I glanced in at the tangle of thick, pink worms wriggling in the black soil and shuddered.

"Summer, the fish love these boys," John added. "If it was fall or winter, we'd be using minnows on the hooks. Water's warm. Means the walleye will be active, more aggressive. Gotta watch yourself."

Father waited as I continued to eye the bait. Finally, I reached in and pinched one of the worms. It protested by wriggling furiously in my hand.

"Don't let him slip away," said Father. "Now, hook it."

I tried to copy what I had seen him do in the past, piercing one end of the worm with the hook and then drawing the length of its body onto it, kind of like pulling a stocking over one's foot and ankle. I'd have been lying if I said it was easy or pleasant. The worm smelled foul, and the hook came through its outer layer several times and I had to rework the hook back in and up through its body. Finally, my hook was baited.

"All right now," said Uncle John. "You're going to cast your line and let the jig sink to the bottom, see?" He demonstrated by pulling back his rod and then quickly "throwing" the end of the rod forward in an arc. The hook and sinker sailed out for several yards and then dropped into the water with a gentle *plunk*. He waited a few seconds then began reeling it in with short, sharp bursts.

"Walleye don't like resistance, see," said John. "So, we've got ourselves a slip sinker which lets the fish take the bait and swim off a bit, thinking he's just caught himself an easy meal. These quick draws attract their attention. If you don't get a bite first thing, cast again. walleye like to catch it on the way down."

Father positioned himself behind me in the boat. I stood in the center and braced my feet, the boat constantly rocking in the gently undulating surface of the water. Father placed his arms beside my own, holding onto the rod just in front of where my hands gripped it.

"All right now, the key is to cast smooth and fast. Smooth and fast." With his guidance, I pulled my rod back a bit and then, copying Uncle John, jutted it forward in an arc. The hook and worm flew, trailing the line behind them. The sound of the line leading out was like a bird song. When the sinker broke the surface of the lake, I glanced over my shoulder. Father was smiling proudly.

"That's the way," he said, nodding.

Once all three of our lines were in the water, we each set our sights on who would catch the first and largest fish. Uncle John bet Father a whole dollar that he'd snag a fifteen pounder, which made Father laugh and shake his head.

It would be thirteen years before the state of Michigan's largest walleye would be recorded at 17.19 pounds and 35 inches long, a record that remains unbroken to this day. But in 1938, the average catch was around ten or twelve pounds, and that was big enough, Father always said.

It wasn't long before the first fish bit and pulled against John's line. Bracing his foot against the side of the boat, he started reeling it in. After an initial quick snap of the line to set the hook, John began the slow reeling.

"Oh, he's a strong one," he said, "got some fight in him. Yes indeedy!"

47

The taut line inched nearer and nearer to the boat, and soon the flailing fish broke the surface. Father expertly scooped it out with the fishing net and held it up for all of us to see. The fish was at least two feet long, not huge but good enough for eating. It's eyes were large dark circles with a lighter ring around them, much larger than some other types of fish in the area. The scales were pale with a hint of yellow along its side and a black tail and fin. Overall, it was quite attractive for a fish.

"You see the way its eyes reflect the sunlight?" asked Father, holding up the net. "That's how it got its name, walleye. It's a pigment that allows it to see in murky water."

"How heavy do you suppose it is?" asked John.

Father hefted the net. "Oh, seven? Maybe eight?"

"Not bad. Not bad a'toll. But you wait and see! I'm just getting started!"

We continued fishing through the morning. Father caught himself a nine pounder. John another seven pounder. I had cast my line three times and was beginning to think the fish knew a girl was on the other end of it when suddenly my line went taut.

"There you go now," said Father propping his rod in the boat and coming to my side. But he didn't take the rod. Instead, he watched me with intense focus. "Give that rod a hard yank to set the hook."

I yanked, and I could feel sudden resistance on the line.

"He's mad now!" said Uncle John.

I began reeling in the line, but it was much harder than I imagined it would be. Though the fish was deep under water so that I couldn't see him, I could certainly feel him fighting for his life, the weight of him pulling against the line in one direction and then another. A couple times my fingers slipped off the handle, and the line let out a few feet before I grabbed hold again and resumed the struggle.

Finally, Father slipped his net under the fish, straining to bring it to the surface. John dropped his rod and hurried over to help. It took the two of them to lift the fish out of the water, its glistening body arching and bending, its wide mouth gaping for oxygen.

"I'd say this monster is 28 inches," said Father.

"At least," said John. "That makes it about ten pounds! Looks like I owe you a dollar, Dorothy!"

Chapter Nine

THE INITIAL EXCITEMENT of catching my first fish soon waned as John, Father, and I sat in our boat holding our rods for one hour, then two. The men were quiet, the silence punctuated with an occasional "Day's gettin' warm" or "Looks like that one got away."

I hadn't realized how focused men could be on just watching the water. Father went through half a dozen cigarettes before he snagged his second walleye. Three hours later, after we'd caught just under a dozen between us, John announced it was time to head back.

"My oh my," said Marigold when Father delivered our cleaned and descaled bounty. It had taken John and Father record time to prepare them at the dock, insisting that scraping guts out of walleye was men's work. I think Father just didn't want to make me sick, but I helped Marigold transfer the fish to the kitchen table where we separated the filets from the bones and then breaded and fried them for supper.

The meal was delicious, the best fish fry I'd ever eaten served with Marigold's famous green beans and ham. I could have kept right on eating if I hadn't gotten so full.

"I'm going to burst!" I exclaimed, leaning back in my chair. Mother finished off her last of three filets.

"I must admit," she said, dabbing her mouth with her napkin, "that was quite a feast indeed. Dorothy, how many of these fish did you say you caught?"

"Just two," I answered, but I was proud of the pair. I'd worked hard for them.

"Well," Mother added with a nod of approval, "you done good. I don't encourage young ladies getting into the men's world, but I admit your father was right in taking you along today. Though you did get a bit too much sun. Your skin is bound to freckle."

"Let it freckle then," I replied. "I'd go out fishing every day if I could. It was so peaceful out on the water, just the call of the birds flying overhead, the water lapping against the side of the boat."

Charles and Alice both chuckled as Marigold delivered bowls of custard for dessert while Alice guided a bottle into Gary's mouth.

"Next time, it'll be my turn," said Charles. "I would have gone today if I hadn't promised Mother a trip into town. So, you really have me to thank for your little adventure, Dot."

Father, his custard untouched, moved to light a cigarette, but after a warning glare from Grandmother, he tucked it back in his shirt pocket. "What about you, Larry?" Father asked Alice. "Have you ever been fishing?"

"Can't say that I have," said Alice. "Though I'm not averse to the idea, if Dottie and I went together." She winked at me conspiratorially.

"Daddy," I said, excited now, "can we all go with you next time you go fishing? Or even hunting. You are going duck hunting next week, aren't you? I heard you tell John that you plan to go to Harsens."

Mother raised an eyebrow. Father's eyes slowly found mine, then shifted to Mother's.

"Nothing's been set for certain," he said.

Grandmother, who had been heartily enjoying her food and had remained silent until now finally chimed in.

51

"A girl? Duck hunting? Don't be daft. Dorothy Ann, clear the table and take the dishes to the sink."

"I can manage, Mrs. Reid," said Marigold. "Besides, Miss Dorothy is probably tuckered out. Why don't you go on to bed? I'll wash up."

"I'll give you a hand," said Alice, handing Gary to Charles.

In a blink, Marigold and Alice had whisked away the dishes, Mother and Grandmother had retreated to the sitting room to knit, and Charles had taken Gary to the back bedroom to lay him down to sleep. Father and I remained at the table. After glancing toward the door to make sure we were alone, he snuck the cigarette from his pocket, struck his lighter, and held the flame to it.

"Thank you for taking me today," I said after a few moments. "It really was an adventure."

Father smiled and took a pull on his smoke. "It was, wasn't it? You caught on quickly. Even John was impressed."

"Really?"

"Really. He told me that now that he knows how little trouble a girl can be in a boat, he just might take his own daughter one of these days."

"I don't know. I have a hard time envisioning Ruth reeling in a two-foot walleye. She is only ten, after all."

Father smiled, amused. "Well, maybe she'll need to grow into it." He tapped the ashes from his cigarette onto a saucer. "It's been a long day," he said. "I think I'll turn in early. Perhaps you'd better do the same."

He crushed out his stub on the saucer, then stood up and pulled his handkerchief from his trousers pocket. He removed his spectacles and wiped the lenses. Before replacing the spectacles, Father closed his eyes and pinched the top of his nose.

"Are you feeling all right?" I asked. I'd seen him do that before in the past, and usually it meant a headache was coming on.

He opened his eyes and looked at me. "I'm fine, Polka Dot," he said. "Just thinking too much is all."

"About what?"

He took a deep breath. "Oh, about you. About Bertie and Chic. You've all grown up so quickly. Seems like only yesterday when your brother and sister were just tikes running along the river's edge. I remember one summer, I suppose Bertie was just five or six and Chic was maybe three. I took them out on the water in an old rowboat. It was a day much like today, clear skies, plenty of birds overhead. We didn't even go far from shore, just paddled around a bit, but they both giggled with delight the entire time. To them, it was a great adventure. Mother stood on the shore, of course, kept her eyes on us. She was convinced with all their wriggling about they'd surely fall in and drown. In fact, you *did* fall in once, and I fished you right out, fussing and sputtering."

Father allowed himself a soft chuckle at the memory.

"So long ago. I doubt any of you remember. But I've thought of it many times over the years. You never forget, you know. Those precious moments with your children. At the moment they occur, they don't always seem so precious. Like those few minutes in the rowboat. It isn't until much later that you realize they are treasures, once the years have passed and your children have grown and forgotten. Then the memories become pearls strung together on a thread."

Father replaced his spectacles and tucked his handkerchief back into his pocket.

"That's why I took you fishing today. Because I've come to realize that you can never have too many pearls."

He bent forward and kissed my forehead. "Good night, Polka Dot."

"Good night, Daddy."

He gave me a gentle smile and then left the kitchen. I listened to the stairs creaking as he went to his and Mother's room, and the soft sound of the door closing behind him. I decided then to never forget that day, to make that pearl of Father's mine too.

Chapter Ten

WALTER AND I set out around nine o'clock Tuesday morning to deliver Florence's leaflets. Alice came with us, leaving Gary with Charles for an hour or two. We decided to start at the far end of Grandmother's neighborhood and work our way back to the house. We took opposite sides of the first street, Walter on one side, and Alice and I on the other. The first house on the corner was a modest single-story home painted white with dark red trim. Alice rapped on the door, and an older man with a grizzled gray beard answered.

"Good morning," said Alice. "I'm Alice Reid and this is my niece Dottie. We're visiting our neighbors to invite you to—"

"Reid?" the man interrupted. "Did you say Reid? Margaret Reid?"

"Uh, yes," I said. "Margaret is my grandmother."

The man nodded his head vigorously and then suddenly disappeared from the doorway. Odd, I thought, preparing to leave and move onto the next house. But from inside, we heard his voice booming: "Emma! Emma, there's some girls out here looking for you! Peg Reid's girls!" There was a moment of silence where we could not hear Emma's response, but she must have said something because the man hollered back. "They don't care if you're not dressed up. Just get out here! I'm having my coffee!"

Alice looked at me as if searching for an answer as to how to handle this. I just shrugged. By this time, I could see that Walter was on his third house. He was chatting with a young mother, a baby perched on her hip, and watching us, curiously, out of the corner of his eye.

Finally, Emma came to the door, a little bit flustered. She was wearing a house coat and a cloth wrap tied over her hair set in curlers. Alice tried again.

"We're inviting everyone to the 4th of July celebration in a couple of weeks. There will be a boat parade, races, food competitions, music, dancing, and fireworks!"

Emma took the leaflet from Alice. "Oh, what fun. Of course, we'll be there. Now that the government's made it a paid federal holiday, my Stan can take the day off for the first time in years. Thank you girls, and tell Peggy, Emma Carpenter says hello. Stan still talks about that cake she brought over when he was down with pneumonia last year."

She gave a friendly wave of her fingers and shut the door.

Alice smiled. "That wasn't so bad," she said as we moved on to the next house.

At the end of the street, we found Walter waiting for us, his stack of fliers significantly diminished.

"I've done the whole next street over already," he said. "You girls like to take your time."

Walter was right. Most of the houses, once we told them we were Reids, wanted to chat for a few minutes. Some of the older couples remembered Grandpa James Reid and spoke highly about him. Others expressed gratitude for Grandmother and Marigold and the baked goods they'd shared. Seems Grandmother kept an eye out for her neighbors and liked to deliver food when there was sickness. While I'd always known Grandmother was kind, I'd never realized how that kindness extended to those outside our family.

Walter took some of our fliers and offered to canvass the next street on his own, but Alice shook her head.

"Nonsense. You've knocked on three times as many doors as we have. Why don't you accompany Dottie this time. You take that side, and I'll take the opposite. I'll try and move a bit faster this time, and I think I'll leave out my last name."

So, Walter and I started a new street. We'd made it through the first four houses with no distractions when we came to one of the nicest we'd come across so far. It was two stories, like the Reid home, with elegant woodwork on a wraparound porch. A man, perhaps in his thirties, was sitting in a chair on the porch wrapped from neck to toe in an afghan. He looked pale, and his hair was disheveled. With his eyes closed, he looked fast asleep. Walter suggested we move along, and I agreed, when the man opened his eyes, pinning us with his gaze.

"What you got there?" he said not unkindly.

Walter and I went up the steps and held out a flier so he could see it. The man's arms were wrapped up in his blanket.

"We're inviting everyone to the 4th of July celebration," I said mustering an enthusiastic smile. The man quietly perused the flier. I could see his eyes following the lines of text.

"Sounds like a grand plan," he said at last. "Wish I had the strength for it." With a sudden lurch, the man began coughing from deep in his chest. At the sound of it, a young woman, presumably his wife, came rushing out the front door. She was thin and quite handsome, with large blue eyes and auburn hair rolled into a bun.

She didn't seem to even notice us as she hurried to the man's side and rubbed his back.

"There now," she said, cooing gently. "It's already passing. There now."

Only once the man's cough had subsided did the woman look up and smile at us. "Doctors say he hasn't got long, but he's a fighter,

57

aren't you, Joseph?"

I saw then the desperation in her eyes, and the hollow emptiness in his. This man was dying. And his wife had not yet accepted the inevitable.

Walter had the sense to speak up. "We just wanted to make sure your family knew about the festivities on the fourth." He handed her the flier. She accepted it but didn't even glance at it. Walter turned to the man. "Hope you feel better soon, sir."

As Walter and I left the porch and headed for the next house, I couldn't help but glance back. The man was calm now, sedate, his wife brushing his hair from his face with trembling fingers. Then she leaned over and placed a gentle kiss on the top of his head.

Walter stepped to the next door and knocked. As we waited, I considered that man's life, how it would be so cruelly cut short. But at least he's got time to say goodbye, I reasoned. Though clearly he was in pain, and it was likely to get worse.

The door opened, and Walter began his spiel about the celebration, but my mind was still on the dying man. Could I, if I ever found myself in that position, endure such suffering? *Would* I?

Nonsense, I scolded myself, pushing the unpleasant thought out of my head. Such decisions are not mine to make.

"Are you all right, Dottie?" The door had closed already, and Walter was looking at me with concern.

"Yes," I told him. "Yes, of course. Sorry. My mind wandered."

"You're tired. We should stop and finish tomorrow."

I shook my and reached for the remaining leaflets, taking them from his hand. "There's only a dozen more. I'll do the next house."

In another moment, I'd completely forgotten about the man on the porch and my ephemeral questions. It would be a long time before the incident would come back to me like some disconcerting déjà vu.

Chapter Eleven

WE'D BEEN IN Algonac a week when it happened. It was not unexpected of course because it happens every year. Yet when the Mayflies hatch, it always brings a sense of dread—and wonder.

Mayfly nymphs live most of their lives in the water, often as long as two years. But when they hatch, or transform into adult Mayflies, they take to the air by the millions, completely infesting the surrounding area. The Mayflies themselves are harmless. Related to dragonflies, they have long tails and delicate vein-laced wings which do not lay flat against the body like most flying insects but are held out like a butterfly's wings.

So it's not so much the individual insect that causes problems in Algonac. It's their sheer numbers. Have you ever been outside in a snowstorm with the flurries of snowflakes swirling all around you? Replace the snow with Mayflies, and that's what it's like in Algonac when the insects hatch and move into town.

We were inside Grandmother's when it happened, thank goodness. Father was standing at the window, smoking and peering out at the river in the morning light while Marigold and I set the table for breakfast.

Suddenly, Father said, "Here they come."

And they came!

Within seconds, the sky outside turned dark as the cloud of Mayflies rose from the surface of the water and flew inland like a massive squadron of tiny aeroplanes. Since our home was so near the riverbank, the swarm of insects reached us in seconds.

"I hope all the windows are closed," said Father coolly.

Grandmother and Marigold looked suddenly panicked and hustled throughout the house to check all the windows and doors. The last thing we wanted was for the infestation to get inside!

Fortunately, all was well.

I joined Father by the window and watched. Of course, I'd seen this phenomenon many times before, but it never ceased to amaze me.

"It's interesting," said Father between puffs from his cigarette, "how they live so long in the water. Content there, with everything they need to survive. But it isn't enough, is it? They must break free from their safe environment, but in doing so they've all doomed themselves. Once they hatch, their days are numbered. Do you know how long a Mayfly lives once it's on land?"

I knew from experience that the Mayflies literally cover every surface in Algonac and swarm like storm clouds in the air, but only for a day or two. Then the creatures die, and their carcasses are everywhere until the wind and nature eventually sweep them away.

Father answered his own question. "Hours. A day. At best, two. But to fly, to greet the sun just once in their lives, to be free, makes the sacrifice worthwhile."

You don't want to go outside during Mayfly season if you can avoid it. Because if you do, you'll quickly be covered in the things, as they seek to perch on any surface available, living or stationary. I got caught outside once shortly after a hatch. I was just six when it happened. Father and I had gone to sit on the shore and watch the sun rise. It was that day that the Mayflies decided to hatch. The vast swarm rose from the river like a mist, and at first I was mesmerized

60

by the beauty of it. Father was on his feet in a heartbeat, sweeping me up into his arms. And then we were running. But Father was no match for the speed of the Mayflies. Instantly, we were encompassed by thousands of the things. I screamed in terror and clung to Father as he leapt up the steps and through Grandmother's front door, all the while brushing the insects off both of us. I was frightened of the Mayflies for years until I was old enough to understand what they were.

Father glanced down at me. "Well, might as well settle in for a couple of days. How about a game of backgammon?"

The day passed sluggishly, the hands of the clock on Grandmother's mantle crawling around its face as if time had decided it had nowhere to go, much like the rest of us. Father and Charles coaxed Alice to watch them play, but she soon bored of it and joined me and Mother in the sitting room to listen to the radio. Grandmother had out her knitting bag and was working on a sweater of yellow wool, ironic in the oppressive heat. We dare not open the windows for fear of being invaded by the insects, and the two oscillating fans in the front of the house did little to assuage our discomfort.

Marigold kept the lemonade coming, which helped a bit, but even she spent much of the day lying on top of her bed fanning herself. All the while, we could hear the low buzz of the mass of insects outside.

I must have dozed off because sometime in the afternoon, when the temperature was close to sweltering, someone shook me awake.

I sat up and rubbed my eyes.

"You have a visitor," said Alice with a gentle smile. She was holding Gary in her arms, and he was quite fussy. I empathized with the babe. Alice told me she was going to give him a cool bath and that my guest was in the kitchen.

Father and Charles had found their way into the sitting room and had fallen asleep, one on the loveseat, the other in Grandmother's favorite chair. Grandmother and Mother, it seemed, had retired to their rooms for their own naps.

I found Walter sitting at the table nursing a glass of lemonade, Marigold fawning over him with a plate of egg salad sandwiches.

"Hi Dot," he said when he saw me.

How had he braved the insect storm? And why? I looked him over. Other than appearing disheveled and sweaty, he seemed none the worse for wear. But I did spy a lone Mayfly perched comfortably in his hair. I plucked it up carefully by the wings.

"A stowaway," I said, then carried it to the back door, opened it just an inch, and tossed the fellow outside, slamming the door shut again before any others could enter.

"I was bored out of my mind," said Walter. "You don't mind my coming over, do you?"

Marigold offered me a sandwich, which I gladly accepted before sitting beside Walter. "I wouldn't have done it," I said. "You couldn't have waited until tonight, when at least they'd all settle down a bit?"

"No, I couldn't. Day's been too long as it is. What are you all doing to keep busy?"

"We're not," I proclaimed trying not to laugh. "I think everyone's fallen asleep, except the baby, of course. It's the laziest day of summer."

We finished another sandwich each, which made Marigold happy. Then she set a large wooden case on the table with a heavy thump.

"Since y'all have nothing to do today, how about you help me polish your grandmother's silver?" she asked, already handing out the cloths. "I do this every year on hatch day. The only thing I can do besides nap and complain."

Marigold opened the box lid revealing an impressive set of silver utensils: forks, spoons, knives, serving wear, even a set of salt and pepper shakers. I'd seen these on occasion when we'd had Easter or Christmas dinner at Grandmother's in the past. But it was a rare privilege to be able to handle them. They were, from what I'd been told, given to Grandmother and Grandfather as a wedding gift from her parents, and someday they'd go to Aunt Hat. Each piece felt heavy in the hand and boasted a bold filigree design on the handle. The silver had tarnished a bit since they'd last been used, so we set to work, dipping our cloths into the polishing cream and wiping off the darkened smudges until the piece shone like a full August moon.

The work did help pass the time, and by the time we'd finished and Marigold put away the box, the sun had gone down. I could hear the men stirring in the front room, the furniture creaking under their weight as they stretched and yawned.

"The bugs are settling," said Walter as we packed away the last of the cleaned silver. "Let's go for a walk."

I followed him outside, tentatively scanning the sky for any trace of the Mayflies. While there were still a few flying around, most had found places to land. In fact, nearly every conceivable surface was covered with them, their wings and tails twitching. Walter and I cautiously strode out onto the porch and down the steps, sweeping aside dozens of the creatures with the sides of our shoes. There was no way to prevent stepping on some of them, there were so many, but others fled to the air on our approach, only to settle somewhere else nearby.

"Hard to believe they'll all be dead by tomorrow night," Walter observed, his hands buried deep in his pockets. "They're such interesting animals."

"Not animals," I corrected. "Bugs."

Walter shrugged. Then he stooped and collected one from the ground. He held it up to me in the palm of his hand. "Look at their wings. Like lace. Like snowflakes. Did you know that they mate in the air? Both males and females have two sets of genitals."

"What?" Heat rose to my cheeks, embarrassed by his use of such a word.

"It's true," Walter continued. "Once they've mated, the females fall back into the water to lay their eggs. The larvae will spend their entire lives, a whole year, in the water until they hatch as adults and take to the air. Then the whole cycle starts all over again."

The Mayfly on his hand took flight. Then Walter and I walked to the tree at the edge of Grandmother's property. Walter leaned his back against it.

"Seems such a waste," I said after a while.

"What does?" asked Walter.

"To live so long waiting to break free of the water only to enjoy it for such a brief time."

"I suppose life is like that. It's never really long enough, at least not for the Mayflies."

The sky overhead had darkened, and Walter and I watched as the last rays of sunlight descended below the horizon. I thought about the Mayflies and about my own life. I was only thirteen with years still to go before I'd break free in my own way as an adult. I wondered if I'd travel to California one day, like Alberta, or go even farther. To England, maybe, or even China. My father's family had ventured out of Canada, but they hadn't gotten very far. As far as I knew, Father hadn't been anywhere other than a few trips to New York on business. But I longed to go places, to do things I couldn't do here at home. Was that wrong of me?

As the sky grew black and the stars came out, I couldn't help but admire the countless numbers of them. Like the Mayflies, there seemed no end to the glimmering jewels in the night sky.

Chapter Twelve

1938 MARKED THE inaugural year of the Algonac Pickerel Festival and Tournament. Of course, it wasn't called that at first. The official title came later, long after I'd left Algonac for good. In the decades that followed that first year, the festival became the annual spectacular for the city, raising funds for charity, boasting boat parades, fireworks, food, and family friendly events of all kinds. But that year, the infant celebration was much simpler. Still, all of us in town looked forward to it with unbridled enthusiasm.

It was the third week of June (having spent the previous week canvassing most of Algonac with Florence's mimeographed announcements) when Walter and I bought vanilla cones in town then stood in front of the local RX to watch Mr. Smith, Walter's father, paint fireworks on the outside of the shop window.

"July 4th Celebration!" read the sign in flourished red lettering. "Enter the Pickerel Contest!"

Florence had excitedly explained that the Lions Club planned to host a city-wide fishing competition. The fisherman with the best catch would win a cash prize. The competition, she said, would draw visitors from outside Algonac to our celebration. "It will be great for business and really put Algonac on the map."

"Pickerel," said Walter with a grunt. "There aren't any pickerel in the St. Clair. Just walleye."

"I've heard my uncle John call them pickerel," I said.

"A lot of people do, and its true both fish are pike. But true Pickerel aren't found in these parts, and I've heard they aren't good for eating."

"I see. Still, it's the thought that counts, isn't it? To have some excuse for a celebration?"

Walter bit into his cone and swallowed, leaving a smear of cream across his mouth. "Of course it is," he said, licking his lips.

We continued down the main avenue and finished off our treats. It was warm out, and I was tempted to buy another.

"Are you going to enter the parade?" I asked.

Walter shrugged. "Maybe. My father plans to display his Sportsman. Maybe I'll go along with him."

"Oh, I wish you would. We could decorate it with flags and streamers and flowers."

"Decorate my dad's boat?"

"Of course! It would be fun."

He thought about it for a moment, and finally nodded. "All right. But no flowers. Talking about boats, how would you like to ferry over to Walpole Island?"

"Why?" I asked. "What's there to see?"

"Well, there's the old Potawa Hall. And the Church of England. And of course, the reservation has lots of Indians. There's the trading post. And I've always wanted to see Tecumseh's grave. Haven't you ever been?"

"Not for a few years now. Father says we should let the natives be. That they aren't relics in a museum to be stared at. What about you? Have you been?"

"Loads of times. The war dancers are really neat."

Father had never been one to gawk at the Indians when they came to town. He respected all peoples, no matter how different they

66

were from ourselves. Going to their reservation felt a little like trespassing.

"I saw one just yesterday," said Walter, "in the marketplace. A chief, I'd say. With his buckskins and everything. He bought himself a phonograph and some records."

"Really? A phonograph. Which records did he buy?"

"Not sure, but he carried it all right out of the store, his expression as solemn as I'd ever seen on an Indian. I suppose he took it back to the reservation."

"What do you suppose he wanted it for?"

"Why does anyone want a phonograph for?"

By and by, we decided not to ferry to Walpole but spent the rest of the afternoon diving off the dock near Grandmother's house. The water was cool and clear as glass. Later, as we lay on the planks to dry, Marigold brought us each a lemonade which tasted as bright and delicious as the sun. Eventually, Walter said goodbye and headed home for lunch. But I stayed on the dock, laying on my back staring up into the pale blue sky.

That afternoon, when the sun had grown too hot, I headed into the house hoping to find Marigold and perhaps some snacks. When the screen door slammed shut behind me, I expected Grandmother to holler at me. Instead, I heard a gentle shhh from the shadowed recesses of the front parlor. I stepped into the room and noted that the drapes were drawn, and I found Alice sitting on the sofa, her head resting against the back of it.

"Sorry," I said. "I didn't know you were in here."

"It's all right," she whispered. "Gary fell asleep in his pram there." She indicated the buggy parked by the floor lamp, which was turned off. "It's getting hot, so I thought I'd maybe catch a short nap myself."

"Where is everyone else?"

"Your father and brother are out who knows where. Probably the boat factory, I imagine. I heard them talking about wanting to sneak a peek at the new models. Your grandmother, mother, and even Marigold are in their rooms resting. Not much else to do on a day like today, I'm afraid."

I supposed she was right. Not to mention that watching a baby must have been exhausting work. I thought I might follow everyone's example and retire to the attic for a nap myself, but Alice lifted her head, smiling at me, and patted the spot beside her on the sofa. So, I joined her there.

We both leaned our heads back and closed our eyes. It felt good, doing nothing—not alone but with someone.

"So, tell me about this Walter," said Alice.

I drew a deep breath. "Walter? I don't know. We're friends. Known each other most all our lives, I suppose. I think his family goes back a couple generations here, at least that's what Grandmother says. She respects the Smiths."

"Your brother told me Walter's father owns a shop in town?"

"Yes. The pharmacy. And he's on the city council." I shrugged. "Walter says it's no big deal."

Alice shifted beside me. "You talk awful casual about him. Your friend."

"What do you mean?"

"Well, the way Marigold goes on about him, I thought you and he were…" We both opened our eyes at the same time, and Alice cast me an embarrassed glance.

"Were what?" I coaxed.

"More than friends," Alice finished.

I was aghast, and my face must have shown it because Alice quickly continued. "That is to say, I didn't assume anything. How

68

could I? You'd never mentioned him to me. I'd never even heard his name until we got here last week. I'm sorry. I shouldn't pry."

"Why ever not? You are my sister now, and aren't sisters supposed to stick their noses into each other's business?" I laughed and gave Alice a gentle jab with my elbow. I hated to see her uncomfortable, especially since over the past two years she'd been more a sister to me than Alberta ever was. Not that I blamed Alberta, of course, but she was so much older than I was growing up that we really didn't have what I would call a close relationship. And now that she was married and had a baby, I didn't even see her very often.

I closed my eyes again. "Besides," I continued. "There isn't much about Walter to pry into. He's a chum, nothing more."

Chapter Thirteen

THE LAST DAY of June was hotter than usual, the air heavy with humidity that collected on our skins like a coat of paint that wouldn't dry. Inside the house was no less warm, though with the shades drawn, it was dark and at least gave the impression of cool. Aunt Florence had bought Grandmother Reid two electric tabletop fans with steel blades. One she kept in the sitting room where Alice tried to keep the baby from fussing too much, and the other was set on a crate on the front porch where the men had gathered to play poker after breakfast.

Father, Charles, Uncle John, and Uncle Harry, who had come up from Detroit with his family for a few days, slumped in their folding chairs at the card table, solemn expressions on their faces.

Aunt Hat had opted to stay at their place for the day, and Harry's wife, Marie, had gone with Grandmother into town. Mother and I chose to share the bench swing at the opposite end of the porch, fanning ourselves with one hand and sipping lemonade with the other.

"Feels like August," said Mother, rolling the cold glass against her forehead. "Early heat wave. Hope it passes."

Not only was it hot, but the air was nearly completely still. Not a breath of wind to stir the leaves in the trees. I dreaded spending an entire day like this and hoped that Hat and John's kids might be willing to swim with me later, as Walter had gone to Mount Clemens with his father to see about buying an automobile. I considered reading *Elsie Dinsmore*, but I didn't even have the energy to retrieve it from the attic, which was the hottest room in the house about now.

Father held his cards close to his chest and contemplated his hand. I recognized the look on his face as one of quiet interest. It meant he liked his hand, that it had potential. He laid one card on the table, and John dealt him another. Then Father tossed two nickels onto the table.

The men only bet nickels when they gambled at Grandmother's. Her rules. "No sense pitting family 'gainst family," she'd say, "or lose more'n one can afford." But despite the rules, I'd caught the men sneaking IOU's into the pile from time to time, promises of larger winnings. Still, it was all fun and games, though you'd never know it from watching them. You'd think the world's entire future hinged on a few colored cards and a pile of coins.

Truth was, something felt different that day, something about the way Algonac had come to a standstill. It was as if the world were heralding a coming storm—and indeed it was.

We all noticed the silver Cadillac when it first turned onto our street. Sleek and shiny as a brand new silver dollar. But when it parked in front of the house, even the men laid down their hands to look.

The driver's side door opened and out stepped a short, squat woman with hair all white, curled and set to perfection. She wore round silver spectacles on her nose and a lilac dress. She shut the car door with a confident slam and perched her fists on her hips, taking in several deep breaths.

"Well, I'm here now," she said with a self-assured grin. "Which one of you fellers gonna fetch my luggage from the trunk?"

I felt Mother stiffen beside me and noted her fingers tighten around her lemonade. There was a distinctive moment of hesitation before she set down her glass on the stand beside her and stood, smoothing down her dress.

"Mother," she said, giving Father 'the look' before heading down the steps to greet our unexpected visitor.

Father elbowed Charles who then leapt up from his chair and bounded off the porch to the car. "Hello Grandma," he said, planting a kiss on the older woman's cheek.

Father took his time leaving the table but also made his way to the car and kissed his mother-in-law.

Clara was born in 1864 in Henrietta, Ohio. Christened Clara Petronella Peabody, a name I've always been fond of, she was seventh of thirteen children. "Smack dab in the middle," I'd heard her say. She'd married her first of three husbands, Charles Noble, in 1882 and had three children, of whom Mother was the youngest. Her third husband's name was Pratt, so even though they weren't together anymore, we often called her Grandma Pratt.

In my favorite photo of her, taken later in the 1940s, she posed alongside her favorite dog and wore a full-length fur coat. She looked absolutely regal.

"Is that my little Dottie?" said Clara coming up the porch steps. I flew into her outstretched arms and allowed her to swallow me in a tight embrace. She kissed the top of my head then held me out from her by my shoulders.

"All grown up, I see," she said happily. "Sprouted a good foot or two since I last seen you."

"Grandma, I just saw you at Christmas!"

"I know it. I know it, but you look so darn tall these days, and ladylike. What have you been feeding this child, Dorothy May?"

Mother forced a smile. "She eats the same as everyone else," she said. Charles lugged Clara's two carpet bags into the house.

"I take it you're planning on staying here with us?" asked Mother.

"Just give me the sofa," said Clara. "I'm only staying for a few days. I just come from your sister Leila Grace's in Mount Pleasant. Stayed on a few weeks there. And I promised to spend the 4th with your brother's widow, Lillian. Now that Frederick Jr. has gotten married, she's all alone in that big old house of hers. Might well we two ladies spend some time together."

Clara spotted the card table and the two men sitting at it.

"John. Harry. Nice to see you both."

"You two, Clara," they both drawled.

"What are you playing?"

"Five Card Draw," said John.

There was an uncomfortable silence as Clara regarded each man through narrowed eyes. "Got room for one more?" she asked.

John and Harry looked at each other, then shrugged and scooted their chairs closer together.

"Charles!" Clara called into the house. "Bring out another chair, and one of them cold glasses of lemonade."

As Clara settled in at the table, dropping a fist-sized drawstring bag of coins onto the table, Mother and I settled back onto the bench swing.

As Uncle John dealt Clara into the game, Mother lifted her lemonade to her lips and peered at them over the glass rim.

"It's nice Grandma Pratt came by," I said, and I sincerely meant it. I loved my grandmother with all my heart and wished I could see her more often. But since Grandpa Charles had died and she'd split with her latest husband, she hadn't stayed in one place very long.

Mother took a sip and ran her thumb down the condensation. "Nothing nice about it," she said with a subtle shake of her head. "Your Grandmother's here on business, that's what. And it's my business she's after."

Chapter Fourteen

WHEN GRANDMOTHER REID returned home from town and found Clara there, she embraced her and invited her to help with supper. The two women had, through the marriage of their children, known each other for ages and got along famously. The two of them split peas at the table and caught up on each other's lives while Marigold and I made chicken salad in the kitchen. Occasionally, one or the other would laugh, and then the other would join in. Once or twice, Mother came through supposedly to check with Marigold about plans for dessert, though I think she wanted to spy on the old women.

"Marigold, I'm going out to pick the strawberries from the garden. How many do you suppose you'll need for the shortcake?"

Marigold told her two pints would do, but Mother's eyes were focused at the table, disapproval on her face. She dared not say it out loud, but I believe she yearned to be included. I nudged Marigold who understood me without my having to speak my thoughts.

"Mrs. Reid," said Marigold, giving me a nod, "why don't you send Charles out for the strawberries. I sure could use another hand in here with the bread rolls. Yours always come out so angel soft. Would you mind showing me how you do it?"

Mother's attention shifted to the kitchen counter. She scrutinized the ingredients that had already been set out: flour, salt, yeast, sugar. "All right," she agreed. "Let me fetch my apron."

The rolls, of course, were indeed divine. At home, she generally preferred Sadie do the cooking, as Mother's kitchen talents were limited, but dinner rolls were her exception. We all feasted ourselves to overfull that night and were glad when the temperature began to fall. By sundown, the air had cooled, and a soft breeze had picked up.

"I'd love a walk by the river," announced Clara after helping to clear the table. "Who's coming with me?"

Alice, of course, needed to tend to Gary, and Charles had already sprawled out in his bed "to digest." Mother declined the offer, so Father and I accompanied Grandma. I was grateful for the opportunity to go outside and breathe in the evening air. Indoors was still a bit stifling.

Clara and Father set the pace, and I followed behind. They strolled deliberately yet slowly, following the path along the docks. I hadn't gone swimming that day as I'd hoped, but my cousins had agreed to join me tomorrow, and I was already planning in my mind how pleasant it would be to dive into the cold water and then sun myself on the wood pier. Maybe Walter would come as well. It would be great fun.

We reached the gate marking the edge of the boat factory, and Father paused to light a cigarette.

Clara watched him with disapproving eyes. Father caught her gaze and coughed on his first draw.

"I'm sorry, Clara," he said with a contrite smile. "I know you don't approve, but we're out of doors, so I didn't think you'd mind."

Clara patted her hair, which had mussed a little in the breeze. "There's something unnatural about filling one's lungs with smoke. My Charles liked his cigars, and though the doctors claimed otherwise, I believe it's what killed him. Cancer of the lungs."

She folded her arms and turned her eyes to the river. "It ate him up, bled him dry like a blossom left out in the sun without water. And how he suffered."

I stood back a bit, listening. I'd seen my grandfather only once while he was sick. He hadn't yet succumbed to it and was just as cheerful as he'd always been. Later, Mother would go see him but wouldn't let me come along. It had only been a few months when he'd passed. I think Mother didn't want me remembering Grandpa that way, but I wished I'd at least been given the chance to say goodbye.

Father held his cigarette between his fingers, his hands braced on his hips. "Charles Noble was a good man," he said. "Named our boy after him."

"Darn tootin' he was," Clara replied. "Too good for this world. Only wish I'd known it before things went sour between us." She glanced up at Father. "You're a good man, too, Bert. You've always treated my Dorothy May proper, and I'm grateful for that. And you been a good father to those kids of yours. Raised 'em right."

Father smiled. "Well, I tried."

Clara laughed, and so did Father. As long as I could remember, they'd always liked each other. I think Father liked Clara more than her own daughter did, though I never understood why. Maybe it's because Father appreciated Clara's sense of humor, her lightness of being. She was content with the world, comfortable with herself, and she made Father feel comfortable too.

Father flicked the ashes of his cigarette into the water. Clara shivered in the cooling air.

"Let's be getting back," suggested Father. "Dorothy would take me to task if I let you catch cold."

Clara rubbed her arms and nodded. Father raised his hand, bringing the cigarette to his lips, but then he seemed to think twice about it and tossed it into the river instead.

"You'd better be taking care of yourself," said Clara as they turned for home.

Father grinned. "Might be a bit late for that," he said with a chuckle. Clara tucked her arm through his and patted his hand. I was struck by the fondness they had for each other. I almost wished I had let them come out on their own, without me tagging along. But then Father caught my eye and motioned for me to come closer. As I did, he slid his free arm around my shoulder and drew me close. Then he kissed the top of my head, and the three of us, all bundled together, took our time getting home.

Chapter Fifteen

THE NEXT MORNING found Charles, Father, John, and Grandma Pratt on Grandmother Reid's porch playing a round of poker. I had woken early to help Marigold with breakfast and was quite surprised to hear Clara tell Father to deal her in. She didn't ask him, mind you, she told him.

When Mother had dressed and come downstairs, she asked me where everyone was since the house seemed so quiet. I nodded toward the front door, and that's where she headed.

Marigold handed me two plates piled high with scrambled eggs and sausages. She took up two more, and we followed Mother to the porch.

She was standing just outside the door, hands on her hips, glaring at the brood of card players who were already so entrenched in their game none of them noticed her. Marigold and I pressed past her and served up the plates. On the food's appearance, the men rallied, thanked us, and dug into their plates like they hadn't eaten in weeks.

"I'll just take a glass of grapefruit juice, if you don't mind," said Clara, her eyes intent on her hand. I picked up her plate to take it away. I had plans to eat it myself.

"Mother." My mother's voice was firm, direct, but not loud. But Clara didn't seem to hear. "Mother!"

Clara glanced up, her face crinkled in a curious smile.

Mother shifted her hands from her hips and folded her arms in front of her. She opened her mouth as if to say something, but then shut it again. Then she rolled her eyes, gave an exasperated huff, and retreated back inside the house.

There was a long history between my mother and her own. I didn't know much of it as I was only fourteen, but my sister Alberta had once told me that Mother often disapproved of Clara's "free spirit," as she called it. Clara had married Charles Noble, and somewhere along the line they had divorced, though they'd stayed friends until he died in 1937. She married William Long in 1910, but it didn't last, and remarried a third time with similar results. In between husbands, Clara enjoyed traveling, coming and going as she pleased. I think that may be why Mother disapproved of her. Mother was far more buttoned-down, not prone to flights of fancy.

I don't know how Mother felt about her parents' separation. She never discussed it, and I never thought to ask. But I imagine it was upsetting to her, that maybe her gravity of character was partly born of it.

I carried my plate into the kitchen and sat down to enjoy it. Marigold came in to squeeze Clara's juice. Mother paced the kitchen for a few moments before joining me at the table.

"Marigold, I wouldn't mind some of those eggs, if you please," she said. Marigold obliged. Mother's plate steamed, and the smell was delicious. We ate in silence, with only the sound of our forks clinking against the porcelain plates. When we were through, Mother offered to clear. I headed outside and collected the men's empty dishes and returned to help Mother wash up.

"What are your plans for today?" Mother asked, handing me a dish to dry.

I shrugged. "Walter and I might go swimming. Maybe go into town later for some bowling."

79

"Sounds fun."

We both heard the creak of the front door open and shut, and in a few moments Clara had joined us in the kitchen holding out her empty glass.

"Nothing quite as refreshing as grapefruit juice," she said cheerily. "Like oil to an engine."

She set it on the sink beside Mother, who I noticed had stiffened. Clara noticed it too.

"Won a dollar off your Charles," Clara said with a chuckle. "He's got to learn to keep a straight face in poker. He's got a tell like a highway sign. Now, Bert, on the other hand, he's a devil at cards, I tell you. Never met a man so sly—"

"Mother, please. That's enough." Mother slapped a soapy hand against the counter. Clara did not act in the least bit surprised.

"What? You don't approve of poker?"

"I don't approve of *you* playing poker. You know that."

"You didn't say anything last night. Even when I won the first hand."

"How could I when I was still reeling from your sudden appearance out of nowhere."

Mother turned from the sink to face Clara who was as cool and calm as always.

"Why didn't you ring ahead?" Mother asked.

Clara gave a little whish of her hand. "I didn't know I was coming until I was on the road halfway here. Made up my mind along the way. What's wrong with wanting to see my daughter and my grandchildren?"

Mother dried her hands on a tea towel. I seemed to have been forgotten.

"Nothing's wrong with that, Mother," she said. "Only this isn't my home. And it wasn't right of you to drop in unannounced."

"Oh, Margaret doesn't mind a bit,"

"I mind!" Mother's voice grew taut. "I do enjoy a visit now and then, you know I do, but this is Bert's home. His family. His river. His town!"

"*His* river? *His* town?" Clara took one step closer to her daughter. "Is there something going on between you two I should know about, Dorothy?"

Mother seemed to remember I was there then, and shook her head, forcing a smile. She turned back to the dishes. Clara seemed to understand this wasn't the time or place to continue this conversation, and I felt suddenly ill at ease. I wished there was some way I could politely withdraw. Why couldn't Walter show up just then rapping on the back door for me? Or Alice call me into the back room to help with Gary?

Instead, Clara quietly exited the kitchen while Mother and I finished up with the dishes.

June 28, 1938

Dear Judy,

My Grandma surprised us with a visit to Algonac. She's one of my favorite people in the whole world. Daring and independent, Clara Pratt lives her life how she sees fit and, like she says, "don't put up with nothing from nobody." She came by my room to say goodnight last night and said the strangest thing.

"Look after your mother," she told me. "She acts stronger than she really is. There comes a time when even a woman like Dorothy May's gotta break apart, and when she does," Grandma added, "you be there for her. You hear?"

I promised I would, of course, and then she kissed me and slipped out of the room. In the morning, she had gone. Packed up her things while we were all still sleeping and went on her way. She's always said she hates goodbyes, so no one was surprised at the silence she'd left behind. But I can't stop thinking about what she said. What do you think she meant by it? Mother is often fierce and unbending. The only times I've ever seen her shed a tear were when she held little Bruce and Gary each for the first time. But those were tears of joy, and within moments, she had shifted into high gear taking charge of things and giving advice. I have a hard time imagining Mother ever breaking apart over anything.

Soon is Independence Day and promises to be a memorable occasion. I hope you have a spectacular celebration in Cleveland as well. After that, we'll be staying here through the end of July. I'll try to write again before then.

Sincerely,

Dottie

Chapter Sixteen

THE FOLLOWING WEEK was a blur of passing out more leaflets, hanging flags from light poles and banners across store fronts, and helping Aunt Florence make hundreds of patriotic pins made of red, white, and blue ribbon to distribute to parade goers. She kept all of us quite busy: Alice, Charles, Walter, myself, and even Mother and Father pitched in. Marigold and Grandmother spent a good deal of time on their sewing machines creating the flags and banners as well as new dresses just for the occasion.

In between all the celebration hubbub, Walter and I found plenty of time for swimming and eating Marigold's endless supply of sandwiches and fresh fruit salads. As the days passed, our skin darkened to a golden brown, and my freckles had multiplied beyond counting. Mother had given up completely in her efforts to keep me out of the sun and even seemed to approve of, as Father had commented, "the healthy glow" in my cheeks.

I woke up on the 4th of July bursting with excitement. I'd had a hard time sleeping that night because I could hardly wait. The sun was just peeking in through my window drapes, so I guessed it was barely six. But I didn't care. I dressed quickly and brushed my hair. Mother wasn't awake yet, but I found Marigold still in her night dress juicing oranges for our breakfast.

"Oh Marigold! I know you're busy, but would you mind braiding my hair? I don't want to wake Mother."

Marigold laughed. "Course I will," she said, rinsing her hands in the sink and drying them on a towel. I pulled a chair away from the dining table and sat myself down on it.

"You got yo'self some ribbons?" Marigold asked, to which I held up two narrow silk ribbons, one of red, the other blue. She used her fingernail to part my hair down the middle and began deftly weaving the strands of my hair.

"Did you braid your girls' hair?" I asked. Marigold had two daughters about my father's age, both with grown children of their own.

"Mmm-hmmm," she said. "My oldest, Josephine? She'd beg me nearly every morning to comb out her hair and braid it. And I did. The younger one wasn't so interested in looking pretty. A tom boy that one was, but every so often, mostly Sundays 'fore church, I'd hold her still and braid her hair while she wriggled and fussed the whole time."

She sighed at the memory. "That was a long, long time ago."

She and her husband had lived in their own place, she explained. That was until her husband died in a boating accident. The girls had grown up by then, so Grandmother and Grandfather had made room for her in their house.

"When your grandpa died, fifteen years ago now, your grandmother and I were a comfort to each other. I don't know what we would have done otherwise. There now," she said, tightening the bow on the second ribbon. "You look all fine and patriotic."

I felt the braids with my hands, satisfied with their perfect harmony. Marigold was so good at it, though I would never say so to Mother.

As if on cue, there was a gentle rap at the back door. Marigold answered it and led Walter into the kitchen.

"You ready?" he asked. He looked dapper in his trousers and white button up shirt with a red and white striped bow tie and matching cap. "We've got to drive the boat up to Marine City to get it in the water for the parade. My dad says he'll let me navigate all the way back to Algonac."

"Splendid!"

The morning sped by and before we knew it, Walter and I were puttering down the St. Clair, waving at the crowds gathered along the shore. As planned, the parade took a short break to award the Civil War veterans with ribbons before the long train of boats continued on to Algonac where we all docked and went ashore to enjoy the festivities. The day was perfect, with the heat from the previous few days having dissipated somewhat. Despite the cooler temperatures, the first booth Walter and I visited was the lemonade stand where we each enjoyed a tall, iced glass of it. Then we headed to the pie tables where we promised Grandmother we'd help set up the place cards.

More than two dozen families had donated pies for the occasion. I spotted Marigold's right off and found Father inspecting the huckleberry pie with a hungry look in his eye.

"You have to wait until they've been judged," Mother said, giving Father a playful smack on his hand when he tried to pinch off a bit of crust. "The Mayor and City Council will be by at noon for it. Then we'll sell off each slice for a nickel."

Father fished in his pocket and poured a handful of coins into Mother's hand. "I claim Marigold's entire blueberry pie for myself." He paused, seeing me and Walter come up beside him. "And for the entire Reid clan."

Behind the table, Marigold beamed with pride.

"You don't have to do that, Mr. Reid," she gushed. "I made you your very own pie and left it on the table back at home. I know how much you love huckleberries!"

Father laughed. "Well then," he said to Mother, "consider that a

85

donation."

Mother rolled her eyes, but she was smiling, and when Father winked at her, I could swear I saw her blush.

Walter and I filled the morning with plenty of activities. We cheered on my cousins in the watermelon eating contest and applauded when Uncle John won second place with his ten-pound walleye in the fishing competition. Marigold didn't win the pie contest. That honor went to Mrs. Perkins' mile high strawberry pie, but her slices were the first to sell out. Even though Father had a pie waiting for him at home, he still bought and ate one slice each of Marigold's pies.

The afternoon rolled on. Walter and I changed into our swim clothes and joined his friends at the docks, splashing and diving in the water, then sunning ourselves on the pier.

At supper time, Grandmother called us all home where we ate brisket and corn on the cob. Alice had laid Gary down for a nap, and the men sat on the porch smoking cigars and talking about the boat races. Walter's father had won two of them, and Uncle John had won five dollars betting on him.

When the sun began to set, one by one, we all seemed to get our second wind and headed back into town, blankets in tow. As we neared the park, I could hear the band playing a rousing rendition of "Yankee Doodle". We spread our blankets out on the grass, along with dozens of other families, and settled in for the evening. Walter found me and asked if I'd like to walk down by the water before the fireworks began. I agreed.

We weren't the only ones with that idea. I spied Father and Mother strolling together along the bank. At one point, she slipped her arm through his.

"It's been a good day, hasn't it?" Walter asked. The river lapped gently against the bank, and I counted more than twenty boats drifting in the water.

"It simply couldn't have been more perfect," I said.

My parents reached a park bench and sat down, Mother's arm still tucked in Father's elbow. I tried to remember the last time I'd seen them sit beside each other so closely.

Walter said, "My Dad's going to Dearborn tomorrow, to pick up some lumber. He's building a new shed in the back yard."

They were too far away for me hear them, but Father and Mother were talking to each other. By the way Mother smiled and laughed, it was likely nothing important. Probably just remarks about the day, but I was mesmerized watching them.

"I'm sorry. Did you say something, Walter?" I said when Walter said my name for the third time.

"Just wondering if you'd like to drive to Dearborn with us tomorrow is all."

"Are you sure? Didn't they just have that grocery strike? Those bombs? Is it safe?"

"That was two weeks ago, and it was over in minutes. Everything's fine now. Besides, it might be fun. We could get some ice cream."

"We can do that here."

The sun had set, and my parents sat in silhouette against the moonlight reflecting off the river. The band struck up "God Bless America", the new patriotic song by Irving Berlin. I'd heard it sung by Kate Smith for Armistice Day in November and had fallen in love with it, just as everyone else had.

When the notes began to play, the first fireworks set off across the river, lighting up the sky like bursts of stars. Walter and I fell silent, and I felt his hand brush against mine before I quickly moved mine to my lap. Had he tried to hold it? I couldn't be sure, but I was pretty certain I wasn't ready for that.

Despite the beauty of the night sky and the music playing, my eyes were on Father and Mother. They could not know that I was nearby watching, or that anyone had anything other than the fireworks in their sites, when Father leaned close to Mother and kissed her.

Chapter Seventeen

"DOROTHY ANN! You have a letter here!"

It had been three days since the 4th of July celebration, and with all that excitement over, summer had slowed to a languid crawl. Grandmother Reid was still in her house dress and slippers that morning as she rapped on my bedroom door so loudly that it reverberated through the entire house. I'd been sound asleep dreaming about Betty, Judy, and I and our first day of the coming of school term.

I yawned and scrambled out of bed. What could be so urgent this time of morning?

"What is it, Grandmother?" I asked, my door squeaking as I opened it. "Is something wrong?"

Grandmother smiled broadly and waved a blue envelope in the air. "Postman's just delivered this. It's from Alberta."

Alberta! My only sister, the oldest in our family, was as close to a celebrity as we would ever get. Before marrying, she'd spent a year in Hollywood as a nanny for a rich family's children. She'd had lots of adventures there and had kept us all informed of them via postcards with pictures of the beach, Groman's Chinese Theater, and Sunset Boulevard. She'd dated a fellow by the name of Tyrone Power for a while who, years later would become a legendary Hollywood actor.

I took the envelope and slipped a finger under the flap to coax it open, but I could tell from Grandmother's expression that she was even more anxious than I was.

"What does it say?" she asked.

I removed a single sheet of paper and scanned over the brief note. "Alberta's coming to Algonac for a visit!"

Grandmother clasped her hands excitedly. "I haven't seen that girl since the wedding. Oh my, so much to do to get ready!" She hurried away toward the stairs but abruptly turned back to give me a firm hug.

"I nearly forgot! Happy birthday, Dorothy Ann."

The morning was punctuated with birthday greetings from Mother, Father, Charles, Alice, and even Aunt Florence, who stopped by to bring me a basket of fresh peaches and to apologize for missing my celebration later that evening.

"The City Council has voted to fund some new books for the library. So, I'm heading to Detroit to the booksellers to make a list of suggested titles. Oh, I'd love to see a few copies of that new children's book, *Mr. Popper's Penguins*. Have you read it, Dottie?"

I hadn't.

"It's really delightful. And I just finished reading a play published a few months ago called *Our Town*. Truly inspiring. I'm sure it will become a classic. Our library will surely benefit from having today's best stories, don't you think?"

I agreed and then wished Florence well before she dashed off on her errand.

I spent most of the day with Walter and my cousins, swimming in the river and sunning ourselves on the bank. Later, after supper, we all gathered on Grandmother's front porch. Mother carried out a beautiful white frosted cake lit with fourteen candles while everyone sang "Happy Birthday, dear Dottie" (though Father nearly shouted 'Polka Dot'). Mother proudly announced that she had baked the cake herself (with guidance from Marigold), German chocolate with coconut frosting, my favorite. I received a stuffed bear with a pink bow from Charles and Alice, several books from Grandmother and Florence, a bouquet of summer blossoms from John Jr. and Ruth, and a brand new pair of saddle oxford shoes from my parents.

"I can't wait to wear them to school," I said, modeling them for everyone to see. I was already imagining the outfits I would wear them with. "Thank you so much everyone!"

Walter waited until I'd finished opening my gifts before he sheepishly announced he hadn't brought a gift.

"Not a *real* gift, at least," he said. He then recovered a package from under the porch swing that I hadn't noticed before. It was wrapped in plain brown paper and string. He held it out to me. "I made it myself. Nothing fancy."

I pulled off the wrapping and discovered a small stack of blank paper. They were bound together with a blue ribbon, and as I flipped through the pages, I realized that each sheet had my name written across the top in brilliant blue ink.

"I tried to match the color of the river," Walter explained. And then, as if I hadn't understood him, he added, "it's stationery. I know you like to write letters. Maybe now you'll write me more often."

The paper wasn't the rough, brown kind they gave us to write on in school. This was higher quality than any I had seen before. I ran my fingers across the letters of my name. I could feel the slight indentation where the pen had pressed into it.

"You wrote all these yourself?" I said, trying to imagine how much time and care had been taken to create this gift. "Thank you." Then I threw my arms around Walter and squeezed him tight. He hesitated with surprise, but then hugged me back.

"All right," announced Grandmother, smacking her hands together loudly. "I'm ready for another slice of cake!"

Chapter Eighteen

ALBERTA AND HAROLD arrived two days later after a half a day's drive from Chicago. They let a room at the local inn and telephoned Grandmother to tell her they were going to get a good night's sleep before coming over for breakfast in the morning. I was anxious to see my sister and had a difficult time falling asleep, even after reading for an hour. But in the morning, I bounded out of bed the moment the sun peeped through my window.

"Morning, Marigold!" I chirped as I swept into the kitchen wearing my best slacks and blouse. "What's for breakfast?"

Marigold was just as cheerful as I was, all smiles and energy. "Flap jacks with cinnamon and apples. Alberta loves my flap jacks. Would you fetch the maple syrup from the cupboard?"

I did as I was told and placed the little glass jug on the kitchen table. Then I set the table for eight. Father had borrowed Grandmother's desk chair and one from the back porch so we could all squeeze around it. Mother had suggested we dine in the sitting room or even out on the porch, but Father said it had been too long since the entire family had had a meal together and were going to do it properly—at a table.

I hadn't seen Alberta, who was fourteen years my elder, since just after little Bruce was born in October. Mother and I had, of course,

93

traveled to Chicago to help the new mother out for an entire week. But Father hadn't seen her since last summer.

Father wandered into the kitchen still in his robe and slippers. His hair was mussed, and he rubbed his eyes and yawned.

"Smells awfully good in here," he said, pinching off a piece from the stack of the steaming flapjacks. Marigold playfully slapped his hand away.

"You'll just have to wait for Alberta to get here like everyone else," she scolded, but she was laughing too.

Father took on the job of squeezing oranges for juice, and I fried up a pile of sausages. By the time the others had awakened, a feast was spread out across the table.

Just after eight, there was a light rap on Grandmother's front door. Grandmother, wearing a smart looking yellow house dress, hurried to answer it while the rest of us congregated in the living room.

Alberta was alone, stepping through the door in a crisp light blue blouse and white slacks. She was tall and slender, with bright blue eyes and lips painted in summer red lipstick. Her light brown hair was swept back in a casual curl.

"Where's the baby?" Mother asked, planting a kiss on her oldest daughter's cheek.

"He's still sleeping," said Alberta. "Harold's watching him. But I just couldn't wait another second to see all of you. Do I smell sausages?"

I threw my arms around my sister who was several inches taller than me. And she gave me a hearty embrace in return.

Charles and Alice happily greeted Alberta and explained that Gary was also still sleeping in the back room, but they'd all have plenty of time to play with the babies later.

Through all the excited greetings, Father stood apart, hands in his robe pockets. Finally, Alberta broke from the rest of us to approach him.

"Dad," she said and slid her arms around him. Father seemed to melt right into her as he enfolded his firstborn into his arms and kissed her temple. He said nothing, but the smile on his face and the moisture in his eyes told me he was beyond thrilled to see her.

Alberta had always been an adventurous soul, heading out to California as soon as she was old enough for Father and Mother to relent. I had lived for all her postcards and wondered how she'd endure "settling down" once she got married and had a baby. But she and Harold were a perfect match, and Alberta had never seemed happier.

"Breakfast is getting cold," Marigold called from the kitchen. "C'mon and eat something."

Alberta and Marigold enjoyed a happy reunion. "Flapjacks!" exclaimed Alberta. "No one makes these as good as you do, Marigold. Why, I'm certain I've died and gone straight to heaven."

Marigold beamed at the compliment, and when she divvied out the flapjacks, she placed an extra one on Alberta's plate.

During the meal, everyone peppered Alberta with questions about the drive up from Chicago, about the baby, and Harold's employment. The ride was "spectacular," Bruce was clever and mischievous, and Harold had recently been promoted.

After the meal, Alberta headed back to the hotel, stating she would meet up with us later. She was here for just for the weekend. Harold could only get a few days off work, enough time to travel to and from Algonac. "But Saturday and Sunday are ours," she exclaimed, waving to us as she climbed into her cream Toyota Phaeton with sleek streak lines on either side. Harold had bought it shortly after their wedding and though it was the only car they owned, Alberta often referred to it as *her* car.

As usual, I helped Marigold with the dishes as she bounced ideas off me for lunch. We finally settled on chicken salad with halved grapes and pecans on a bed of iceberg lettuce. That meant a trip to the market for the produce.

"I'll pick them up for you, Marigold," I offered. "Alberta will want to go into town. I'm sure she wouldn't mind."

"Well, in that case," she replied, "I'll make you a list."

Grandmother kept money in an empty jam jar for Marigold's grocery shopping, and from it she withdrew two quarters.

"A head of lettuce is seven cents, walnuts about nineteen cents a pound. I don't need that much. Just get me a quarter pound."

She added up the cost of grapes and added in a pound of bacon for the next day's breakfast. That tipped the total past what she'd given me, so she gave me another quarter. All I had to do was wait for Alberta to return.

I was sitting on the front porch reading, trying not to melt in the heat of the day when Walter came by whistling. He wore pants cut off at the knee and a ratty shirt with the sleeves rolled up to his elbows.

He perched one foot on the bottom step and peered up at me. Like me, his face and arms had darkened a shade or two from the sun in the month since I'd arrived.

"What are you doing?" he asked.

"What does it look like I'm doing?" I answered, flipping a page in my book.

"Looks to me like you're wasting a perfectly good morning. We could go fishing at the canal. Or just put our feet in the water."

"Tempting," I said, "but I'm waiting for my sister."

He shifted his feet, placing his other on the step and the first on the ground. The sun was in his eyes, and he squinted.

"Alberta's here?"

I nodded. "We're going to town later. I've got to pick up some things from the market for supper."

Walter stood there, still squinting. Finally, I closed my book and sighed. "You want to come with us?"

He perked up. "Sure. Got nothing better to do."

"Not even fishing?" I teased.

Alberta returned just before noon with Harold and baby Bruce in tow. Bruce was a chubby, babbling eight-month-old and immediately charmed both Father and Mother. Father sat on the porch blowing bubbles against Bruce's cheek and making him giggle. Mother hovered nearby, tickling his tummy. I don't think I'd ever seen a bigger grin on Mother's face.

Marigold was quite smitten as well, but the day was growing hotter, and the hour was quickly passing.

"Don't forget those things I need," she reminded me loud enough for all to hear.

"Oh, do you need to do an errand?" asked Alberta, fanning herself with a paper Chinese fan she'd brought with her.

"Marigold's making chicken salad for lunch, and Walter and I offered to run to the market."

"I'll take you," she offered gleefully. She turned to Harold, who was deep in conversation with Charles making comparisons between Father's Lincoln and the Toyota. Something about horsepower and torque.

"Harold, I'm running into town. Do you need anything?" Harold didn't say a word, just grinned. Alberta laughed. "Yes, I'll pick up some ice cold colas. I can see you need one."

Harold confirmed her comment by wiping the sweat from his forehead with a handkerchief, then went right back to his conversation.

"Father, would you like to come along?" she asked. "I'm sure Walter doesn't want to be the lone male along on a shopping trip."

Father handed Bruce to Grandmother, and in a few minutes the four of us were zipping along in Alberta's fancy car.

The market had a few patrons milling about when we arrived, but Alberta swept in like a movie star entering Saks Fifth Avenue, which had just recently opened in Beverly Hills (Alberta kept up with Hollywood news). Though she'd practically grown up in Algonac, she acted as if she were a celebrity. And in a way she was.

"Well, if it isn't little Bertie Reid!" exclaimed the store owner, coming round the counter to give my sister a hug. Mr. Reiser was in his sixties with thinning gray hair and a rotund belly striped by bright red suspenders.

"How are you, Mr. Reiser?" Alberta asked, giving him a dazzling smile.

"Not too bad, not too bad. Better now that I've seen a familiar face." He turned to Father. "Why didn't you tell me your daughter was coming to town? I might have put up streamers or a sign at least." He turned back to Alberta. "Welcome home, Bertie," and kissed her cheek.

Alberta hadn't been to Algonac in several years due to her time in California, her marriage, and then having a baby. So, I wasn't surprised at the happy reception. Through it all, Father beamed proudly.

We collected the items on Marigold's list, and then Alberta added a few things of her own: fragranced bath salts, some honey for Grandmother, and a rose scented candle.

"I love lighting candles when I bathe," she explained. "Transports me to another world."

After the market, Father suggested we go to the drug store for sodas. We all agreed that sounded perfect for hot day like today. The store felt cool with two ceiling fans turning, and we took four stools at the counter. Father ordered root beer floats all around. The clerk took four glasses down from his shelf and plopped a scoop of vanilla ice cream into each, then topped them off with bubbling soda from the jerk and shot straws into them.

I pulled my glass close and sipped. The cold frothy treat tasted so sweet and creamy, I actually uttered "Mmmmm". Walter laughed, but when he tasted his, he did the same.

"I wish you could see the outdoor soda fountain in Beverly Hills," Alberta said when she was half-way through her float. "Mary Pickford owns a miniature golf-course, and the soda fountain is marvelous."

"Outside?" asked Father, surprised.

Alberta nodded and took another swallow of Root Beer. "The weather is so nice all year round. Rarely rains, you know. California *is* the Sunshine State. Someday," she added, directing her comments to me, "maybe I'll make it back there, and you can come with me. Wouldn't that be fun?"

I said yes, it would be fun, though honestly getting all the way to California seemed like a fantasy. I couldn't even imagine Alberta going back anytime soon, not with a baby.

Once we'd drained our glasses and resisted the temptation for another round, we headed home and delivered Marigold's groceries. She commented on the late hour and how little time she had left to prepare lunch, but she wasn't really upset. She just wanted everything to be perfect for Alberta's visit.

While Mother and Grandmother fussed alongside Marigold in the kitchen, and Charles and Alice took Gary on a walk in his pram, Father and Alberta sat outside on the porch. I wanted so much to join them, but they hadn't seen each other in a long time, and I felt they should have some time to themselves. I sat in the sitting room intending to listen to the radio, but with the front door open, I could hear their voices through the screen, and curiosity got the better of me.

Father asked Alberta about Chicago, and she remarked that it was a city. Lots of excitement and things to keep her busy, much like California in that way. But at the same time, she'd missed the quiet solitude of Algonac.

"We weren't planning to come up," she explained, "but the more I thought about you all being here, the more I wanted to join you."

Father listened in his unobtrusive way. I heard the strike of his lighter and visualized him lighting a cigarette. Then the lighter struck again. Alberta had likely accepted a cigarette from Father.

"I know you don't approve," she said with a little laugh.

"You're an adult," Father replied.

"You didn't approve of a lot of things, like going to California and marrying Harold."

There was a pause before Father spoke again. "I'd say it was your mother who didn't approve, though it was more that she was concerned. And we both like Harold immensely, you know that."

The porch swing creaked as they sat down on it.

"But you never said that you *did* approve, so I assumed…"

"You were eighteen, Bertie. And Hollywood seemed like such a great adventure," said Father.

"It was an adventure."

"Who was I to stand in your way?"

From the kitchen I heard the *scrape, scrape* of a potato being peeled and Grandmother ordering Marigold to turn down the heat on the chicken.

Outside, Alberta continued.

"I suppose I just wanted to hear you say that you approved of my decisions. Mother's always been quite vocal about how she feels. If she doesn't like something, she lets me know it in no uncertain terms. And when she compliments me, which is rare, at least I know she's in earnest. But you're different, Dad. You've always been hard to read, like a book with a lock on its cover."

I couldn't help myself but peak out through the screen. What was

Alberta up to? Why was she being so frank with Father? He didn't deserve to be cornered like that.

I couldn't see much from where I stood, but the two of them sat side by side on the swing. Father leaned forward, bracing his elbows on his knees, his cigarette perched in one hand.

"I didn't intend to be so cryptic," he said.

Alberta tucked her feet under her. "I suppose we just don't understand each other as well as we might have," she said. "I'm more outspoken, like Mother. Dottie's more like you, I suppose. Introspective. Thoughtful. There's nothing wrong with that, of course, but sometimes it's nice to know what you're thinking."

Father sat up and took a drag from his cigarette and then crushed it out on the swing's armrest.

"Bertie, you're a strong woman who knows her own mind. But I want you to know that I'm proud of you. I've always been proud of you."

There were no more words after that, at least none that I could hear since I stepped back from the door, but I could imagine Bertie smiling, maybe even dabbing at her eyes. Is that why she'd come to Algonac? To coax Father into approving of her? And what did she mean I was like him? Of course, I was like him. Or at least I wanted to be.

I heard the clatter of mixing in the kitchen, the sound of a knife chopping something on the cutting board, onions or maybe celery. The smell of lunch wafted into the room and made my mouth water.

"Dorothy Ann," Grandmother hollered, "call everyone into lunch."

I reluctantly opened the screen door and did as I was told.

Chapter Nineteen

"BERTRAM REID, WHAT have you gone and spent money on?"

Mother, having just finished dusting the lamps for Grandmother, untied her apron as Father came through the door with a big grin on his face.

He'd left early that morning for Detroit with Uncle John, Charles, and Harold to look for a new car to replace John's old Roadster. Mother, Hattie, Florence, Alice, Alberta, and I had spent the morning beating carpets out on the front rail and managing the seasonal deep clean of the Reid house. By the time the men returned, the women were taking a break. Hattie had taken her kids into town for a late lunch, and the rest of us were trying to cool off on the porch.

As Father came up the steps, Mother instantly turned a suspicious eye on him.

"How do you know I spent money?" he asked, planting a kiss on her cheek.

"Well, for one thing, your looking so chipper is a rarity," said Mother, draping her apron across the back of chair. "And for another, you're carrying that box."

Father was indeed carrying a box, though it wasn't very big. Maybe six inches across and four deep. Father set it on the table and beamed proudly at Mother.

"I've been wanting one of these since it came out two years ago. When I saw it for sale today, I couldn't resist."

Father opened the top flap of the box and retrieved the object inside, which he held with such care it might have been mistaken for an antique relic. But this relic wasn't antique. It was sleek and black with shiny silver metal pin stripes across it. Father held it up and then slowly opened the gadget revealing a complicated looking lens.

"A camera!" I said enthusiastically.

"Not just any camera," said Father. "A Kodak Bantam Special."

Mother crossed her arms. "What do we need a camera for?"

But I could see the interest in her eyes as she leaned in closer to have a look.

"To take pictures, of course," said Father. "The one I had when Dottie was little broke years ago. Look at this smooth clam shell design. And it's so compact, I can carry it in my pocket. I've already loaded it with film. It takes 828. Let's go outside and try it out."

Marigold, who'd been overseeing our cleaning, oohed and ahhed as we followed Father across the lawn. Gary and Bruce were both asleep in their prams, so Alice and Bertie snuck away with us too.

"Did John find his car?" Grandmother asked. Father explained that they'd stopped by two car dealers but in the end John had opted to keep his Roadster after all.

"Polka Dot," Father instructed, "you, Bertie, and mother stand over there by that tree."

We did as we were told, and Mother set her hand on my shoulder for the pose as Father took our picture and advanced the film for the next shot. Next, he took a picture of Marigold and Grandmother.

"Let's get one of the couples," Father said. "Larry, you and Chic go first."

Alice and Charles got into place.

"Dad, don't tell me you're still calling Alice that dreadful name?" said Alberta as Father snapped another shot.

"I really don't mind," said Alice. "Having your father christen me with a nickname makes me feel like part of the family."

Finally, Father took the last picture of Bertie and Harold. "Should save some exposures for later," he said, slipping the beautiful machine into his pants pocket. "One roll of film only has room for eight frames. What do you think?"

"What about you?" I asked. "Can I take a picture of you?"

Mother guffawed. "Cameras are expensive. They're not toys for children."

But Father smiled warmly and waved me over. As he drew the camera back out of his pocket, he gave me some advice. "Hold tight to it. It's a bit slippery. I'll set the lens for you so all you have to do is press a button."

He showed me how the front of the camera opened, and then he held it up to his eye, peering through the viewfinder. He turned the dial around the lens, lining up the little numbers, and pointed it at the porch. "There," he said. "That should do it. I'll go sit on the steps there. Wait until I'm in position, then press this button right here. Don't touch anything else, all right?"

I agreed, and he hurried over to the steps and sat down. He took a few seconds trying out different poses and finally settled on resting an elbow on one of his knees. He stared into the camera, a serious expression on his face, as if this was the most important photo he'd ever taken. I couldn't help but think how handsome he looked. There was an old photo of the whole Reid family hanging in Grandmother's parlor. Father was in his early twenties when it was taken. He was dashing then, and full of life and vigor. Now, as I spied him through the camera lens, he looked older. Creases marked the corners of his eyes, and there was a tired look about him. But then, suddenly, his lips curled into the slightest hint of a smile, and for that moment, I saw him as a young man again.

I pressed the button, freezing that image in time.

On Sunday, Alberta, Harold, and baby Bruce came by after church services.

"It's hot as hades out there," said Alberta, whooshing in through the front door in wide-legged navy slacks and the cutest sailor style blouse. She carried a towel rolled under her arm. "How are you all not in the water right now?"

Alberta tipped her sunglasses down and peered at me over the rims.

Father, who was lounging on the sofa reading his paper, peered back at her. "I'm up for a swim. How about you, Mother?"

Mother rolled her eyes. "I'd fry like a catfish in this sun."

"Wear a hat," said Father. I spotted the hint of mischief in his expression.

Grandmother proclaimed she'd prefer to stay indoors until sundown, and Alice said she planned to nap with Gary.

"Why not lay the babies on a blanket in the shade?" Alberta suggested.

Harold, as though he'd planned this all along, held up a folded quilt. "I've got a bit of a cold coming on, so instead of swimming, I'll rest alongside the boys."

"There, you see?" said Alberta. "Who's coming then?"

Charles announced he'd love to take a dip, and Alice quickly agreed.

Didn't take ten minutes for us all to change into our swimming suits and follow Alberta down to the pier. She'd changed as well. Hers was a new style, belted blue shorts and a white halter. She looked magnificent. Mine was a pink one-piece that cut straight across my hips. Father looked dashing in his black trunks and top with narrow shoulder straps. He'd been a team swimmer in his school days, and despite being in his fifties now, the evidence of his strength was still visible.

Charles was the first one in the water. He took a running leap off the pier and cannonballed in, sending up a geyser that sprayed the rest of us. Alice and I were a bit more timid, giggling while dipping our toes in. Father had brought his camera with him and set it on his towel a safe distance from the water.

He followed Charles' example and dove from the pier. When he surfaced again, he was smiling, as if the water and sun had chased away any thoughts outside of the moment. He playfully splashed Charles, who was floating on his back.

"When are you two ladies going to join us?" Alberta loomed over me and Alice, still standing on the bank. She reached out both her hands. Alice and I stood up and each took hold of one.

"Ready?" Alberta asked.

"Ready," I replied.

"I'm not so—" Alice started, but then Alberta made a sudden dash down the pier, pulling me and Alice along with her. Alberta released our hands just as she sprang from the edge of the wooden planks, spearing the water feet first.

I followed without hesitation, and then came Alice with a squeal of delight and a jolly splash.

The water was cold, colder than I had anticipated, but the initial shock of it was quickly dispelled by the intense heat in the air. Immediately, I felt my cares melt away as we all laughed and splashed each other.

For the next hour, we took turns showing off different dives and jumps. Alberta won the silliest award for leaping in while holding her nose, her legs splayed out like a chicken. I couldn't stop laughing at the sight. A boat full of people happened to pass by and applauded. Alberta stood on the pier and took a bow.

Eventually, we all climbed out of the water to lay on our towels.

Bruce and Gary—and Harold—had all slept soundly through the fun. Father took up his camera and snapped a few shots of them slumbering in the shade.

"Here, Dad," said Charles. "Let me take one of you."

"Don't waste film on me, Chic," Father replied off-handedly, but Charles was insistent. Father finally relented. He stood up and posed on the pier, the water in the background. He didn't look at the camera but instead turned his gaze upriver. The laughter and smile were replaced with an expression that was hard to read, as if his thoughts had drifted far away. He looked serene.

Charles took the picture. Father remained standing there for a few moments. As I watched him, I wondered what he was thinking. I wanted so much to be wherever he'd gone just then, to share that place with him. But then he looked back to us lying on the pier and smiled.

"Mind putting the camera in its case," he told Charles. "I suppose Mother will be expecting us home for supper."

We gathered up our towels. Alberta donned her sunglasses again, and we all headed back home. It had been one of the best days of summer so far, though once we'd all dried ourselves and dressed for supper, the day's energy dispelled into a sort of inevitable melancholy. No one mentioned that Alberta, Harold, and the baby would be leaving in the morning, and it would likely be months before any of us would see them again.

Chapter Twenty

"I'M GOING TO boat with John over to Harsens Island. Would you like to come along?"

Alberta had been gone three days during which neither Father nor Mother had said much at all—to each other or to anyone else. It was clear they missed her. But this morning, Father had on his red and black checked hunting cap, which was a good sign that he planned to bring home a duck or two for dinner. He sat outside on the porch inspecting Grandpa's old shotgun and buffing it with a cloth.

"Are you sure that thing still works?" asked Mother from the other side of the screen door.

Father returned her skepticism with a look of incredulity. "Don't doubt Dad's Browning, Dorothy. It never failed him." Then he turned back to me. "You and Walter could putter around the island, if you like. Do some exploring. We'll be back for lunch, I expect."

He was inviting Walter too!

I telephoned Walter's house and told him the good news, and within twenty minutes, the three of us were climbing into Uncle John's boat. Marigold had sent a basket of sandwiches, just in case, she'd said. I helped myself to an egg salad on rye before we'd even started across the river.

The St. Clair is about a third of a mile wide, and in years past, we would often take our car by ferry to Harsen's Island, but today we boated into the dock and dropped Father and John off with their guns.

"Meet us back here in two hours," Father said. "And don't get into any trouble."

I watched as he and John turned inland and started for the marsh, where ducks like to hide in the tall, willowy grasses. Father loved hunting, though it was more of a getaway for him, a chance to focus on nature and enjoy the sunshine. He'd likely shoot a token duck or two just to please Mother and to justify his morning out.

"What do you want to do?" The boat bobbed in the gentle current near the dock. Walter's hand held steady at the wheel. But there was no question what I wanted to do, and he read it in my eyes.

"Tashmoo it is," he said with a broad grin, then motored away from the dock.

Tashmoo Park shared the same name as the Tashmoo paddle steamer that first launched in 1899. The park itself had been around since 1897. The Tashmoo steamer, which I had ridden only once when I was very young, struck a rock on June 18, 1936 and took on water. Though she made it to Amherstberg where all 1400 passengers safely disembarked, the Tashmoo sunk in about eighteen feet of water. Efforts to recover her were unsuccessful, and eventually, she was tugged to a dry dock and broken down for scrap. Since then, attendance at the park had started to decline. The steamer had been the main mode of transportation from the mainland, delivering thousands of visitors to the flats from as far away as Detroit. In fact, President Theodore Roosevelt himself had once ridden on the Tashmoo. But now park goers had to arrive by car via the ferry or by their own boats.

Walter and I traveled in silence, enjoying the beauty of the day: the sapphire water, the waving green trees on shore, the smell of sun in the air. It wasn't long before we reached the Tashmoo dock, an expansive wooden pier as long as the former steamer itself. Walter maneuvered our craft against the pier and tied her up before cutting the engine. Then he clambered out and lent me a hand so I could follow.

"We don't have much time," he reminded me. "Shall we make a run for it?"

We did. Giggling all the way across the covered bridge connecting the dock to the island, Walter and I ran. He was a bit faster than me, and he pulled me along, coaxing me to keep up. Soon, we reached the park entrance completely out of breath. We paid our fare and hurried inside. The park was bustling with people, and the sound of children laughing filled the air. Band music played, the bright, gleeful notes of modern Swing carried along the air from the dance hall, interwoven with the jubilant melody of the Merry-Go-Round.

We couldn't resist climbing aboard the ride, each of us mounting a horse painted in vibrant colors and posed as if trotting along a parade route. As our mounts elegantly strode up and down in circles, Walter and I laughed and laughed. We were the oldest riders, except for the occasional parent there to comfort a frightened child. It was so much fun, we rode it two more times, and by the time we finally disembarked, we were both deliciously dizzy with delight.

"How 'bout some cotton candy?" Walter asked, spying the cart nearby. We hurried over and watched the vendor spin two paper cones around a large metal bowl, pink puffs of sugar clinging to them like clouds. Once our cones were heavy laden with it, Walter paid the man and we set off for more adventures.

Father told me about the first time he'd seen cotton candy in 1908 at the New York World's Fair. He and Mother were engaged at the time and had taken a weekend to attend. Of all the magnificent inventions and artwork displayed there, the most memorable for him had been the fluffy sweet treat.

Walter and I strolled through the park, pulling off the sticky candy and licking our fingers in between. The day was growing hotter, and I was looking for a lemonade stand, when we spotted the Indian tepees and tables lined up beneath the trees offering all kinds of goods for sale to the tourists.

Beaded necklaces and bracelets, leather belts and wallets, little figurines carved from wood, and of course plenty of souvenirs with the name "Tashmoo" painted on them. I'd collected plenty of treasures from the park over the years and wasn't really interested in anything new. Besides, I hadn't brought much money with me. Just enough for the ticket in and some food. But Walter insisted that we browse a bit, so we did.

We came across one table laden with rings of all kinds: copper, silver, polished stone, and glass.

"Why don't you try one on?" suggested Walter. They were all so beautiful, some in the shape of little animals like birds or dolphins, others with intricate blossoms. Still others were simple, yet the colors of the gems alone were decoration enough. I selected a silver band with a geometric design carved into it that reminded me of the ornamentation painted on some of the teepees and slid it onto my ring finger. The fit was perfect.

"I'll take that one," Walter told the Indian seller, reaching for his wallet.

Quickly, I slipped off the ring and returned it to the table. "No," I said. "No thank you. Sorry," I added, apologizing to the man. Then I hurried away.

Walter followed me. When we'd walked several yards, he took hold of my arm to stop me. He turned me to face him.

"What's wrong?" he asked. "Didn't you like the ring?"

"I didn't bring enough money for a ring, Walter."

"I know that. I wanted to buy it for you."

"That's very generous but not necessary. Really. Let's go back to the Merry-Go-Round."

Walter didn't move. He was staring at me intensely. Something was on his mind.

"Dottie," he said haltingly, though I'd never before known him to be short on words. "I *wanted* to buy you that ring."

I tried to understand what he meant. Clearly, from his suddenly serious tone, this was about more than a silly ring.

"But I've got plenty of rings, I really don't need another—"

Walter hastily reached for my hand and grasped it in both of his. They were warm and soft, gentle. A strange feeling shot through me, much like that first day I'd found him fishing at the canal. I was so startled, I found myself unable to pull away.

Walter's expression softened. "We've been friends our whole lives, Dottie," he said. "And the truth is, when you're gone, you're all I think about."

He drew my hand against his chest, and I felt his heart beating. "Tell me, haven't you ever wanted more than friendship?"

He paused, waiting for an answer. Walter. *My* Walter, asking for more than mere friendship. But no, I hadn't ever wanted that. Not with him. Not now. But how could I tell him that? He so clearly cared for me, how could I disappoint him? But I couldn't lie to him either, nor could I lie to myself.

I gently pulled my hand from his grasp and tried to smile. "Oh, Walter," I said, "you've let the day get to your head. We're just here for a bit of fun."

"But Dottie," he continued earnestly, "you're going home soon, so I need to say this." He drew a deliberate breath and said, "I love you."

Now he'd gone and done it. Love. Of course we loved each other, as close friends always do. What could I say to make him understand?

I glanced up at the sky. The sun was now directly overhead. "It's past noon," I said. "We'll be late meeting Father and Uncle John."

Then I spun around and ran for the dock.

"But Dottie!" I heard Walter calling after me, but I couldn't answer. I was already in the boat by the time he caught up. We said nothing more as Walter steered for the flats where we picked up the men. Father proudly showed me the two ducks they'd shot. He and John chatted happily about their day's adventure, seemingly oblivious to Walter's and my silence, though Father cast me an occasional questioning glance.

Chapter Twenty-One

THE SOUND OF Uncle John's boat motor purred across the St. Clair like a contented lion. The river, though ever moving, seemed still and calm today, the currents beneath her surface invisible to the eye.

John's bragging about the ducks tapered to a comfortable silence, and we all turned our faces toward shore.

As we neared, John piped up. "Let's grab lunch at Sid's. I'm famished. What about the rest of you?"

Sid's was a riverside eatery that had been a staple in Algonac for as long as I could remember. What patrons liked best was the dock where boats could tie up right alongside it. Food could be ordered and delivered right to your boat.

Father agreed that he too was hungry, and I had to admit so was I. While I was certain Marigold would whip us up some more sandwiches the moment we got home, the idea of biting into a freshly grilled burger from Sid's made my mouth water.

"I have to get home," said Walter, avoiding my eyes. "Mother's waiting for me to help with chores. But I can walk home from the dock."

"Nonsense," said John. "I'll just drop Bert and Dottie off to place our order while I run you back to Point Duchene."

A few minutes later, Father and I had climbed out of the boat onto Sid's dock and waved goodbye to John and Walter, though Walter had turned away and didn't wave back.

We found an empty table outside and sat down. We didn't even need to look at the menu as we'd been there so often over the years and tended to order the same thing every time, though there wasn't anything on the menu I didn't like.

The waitress was a slender woman in her thirties with dark hair rolled and pinned beneath her cap. She wore a white short-sleeved blouse with a pink skirt and blue apron. Her tag said *Rose*.

"We'd like three cheeseburgers, everything on them, medium rare," said Father. "With fries," he added with a grin.

Rose jotted the order down on her notepad. "Drinks?" she asked. Father looked to me.

"I'll have a sasparilla," I said. Mother so rarely indulged my love of soda pop, claiming it would rot my teeth, but Father's eyes twinkled at my request.

"Make that three."

Rose nodded and collected our menus, then headed inside to get our order started.

Father and I sat quietly for a while, watching the birds overhead. Finally, he broke the silence.

"Walter seemed in a hurry to get home. Is everything all right?"

I should have known Father would see right through me. He had a way about him, as if he was endowed with a sixth sense that could hone in on people's feelings even though they said nothing. I think it was because he was so introspective himself. He understood that emotions didn't always need words to be expressed.

"Did you two argue?" he asked.

"No, we didn't," I said. "In fact, today was one of the best days all summer. We were having a wonderful time, before I spoiled it."

"*You* spoiled it?"

I explained how Walter and I had enjoyed the Merry-Go-Round

and cotton candy, and how we'd been browsing at the gift tables. When I got to the part about the ring, I hesitated to continue, wondering if talking about what happened was somehow a betrayal of Walter's trust.

"Go on," Father gently coaxed.

"Well, Walter said he loved me."

Father tilted his head down a little, his gaze moving from me to the table. A slight grin appeared on his face.

"I see," he said.

"But I didn't let him say anything more," I was quick to add. "I don't feel the same. We're such good friends, and clearly I must have said something, did something, to give him the wrong impression. And now everything's ruined."

Father lifted his eyes to mine. They were so full of understanding, of patience. I wanted to just climb into his lap, like I did when I was little, and let him rock me to sleep. How I wish I were still young enough that his embrace would cure any sadness or fear.

Father reached into his pants pocket and fished out his lighter and his cigarette case. He took his time removing a cigarette and lighting it before pulling a long draw from it.

"Seems to me Walter'd been holding that in for a while now," he said finally. "Takes courage for a boy to tell a girl he loves her. A lot of courage."

I wasn't sure what to say to that.

"I told a girl I loved her once," Father added.

That surprised me. "You mean Mother. Before you were married?"

"No, it wasn't your mother. What I mean is she wasn't the first. I was fifteen, just a little older than Walter. I'd had my eye on a girl at school all year. We were friends, not like you and Walter, of course. I'd only known her a short time, but we sat together in class and sometimes studied together. I was completely smitten."

116

He smiled at the memory.

"In any case, one day after school, after days of deliberating with myself about it, I finally told her how I felt."

"You did?" I asked, engrossed in Father's story. "What did you say?"

"I'd picked a lily from my mother's garden and presented it to her during our lunch hour. I couldn't bring myself to speak to her, so I'd written a note. Said something along the lines of 'You are more beautiful than this flower. Love, Bert.'"

Father went silent and took another draw from his cigarette. A black tern landed on the rail not far from us and paced impatiently as if expecting us to toss it something to eat.

"Well, what happened?" I pressed, eager to hear the rest of the story.

Father shrugged. "Nothing really. She avoided me after that. I think I embarrassed her. And it took many years before I was that brave again, when I proposed to your mother. But that didn't take much courage as she'd told me flat out on more than one occasion that she expected to marry me."

He chuckled.

Rose came out of Sid's carrying a tray and dealt out our burgers, fries, and drinks.

"It's a beautiful day to dine al fresco," she said, indicating the bright blue sky overhead. "If I can get you anything else, just holler."

Then she stepped to the next table where a family of four had sat down. I hadn't even noticed their arrival, I'd been so wrapped up in Father's story.

I pinched a French fry and bit into it. Hot and crunchy with just the right amount of salt.

"I think I felt a little like that girl," I started. "Not embarrassed, but unprepared. I never expected Walter to say such a thing to me. It's changed everything between us, and that's what I never wanted

117

to happen. Things have always been so—so comfortable."

Father ate a fry and took a sip of his soda. "But you see, love isn't comfortable," he said. "In fact, it's downright uncomfortable at times, even painful. Love is about taking risks and being vulnerable, and that means sometimes being disappointed or getting hurt."

"But that doesn't make any sense."

"No, it doesn't, does it? But that's the way it is." He stubbed out his cigarette in the ashtray on the table. In the distance I heard the familiar purr of John's boat coming nearer.

"I've gone and made a mess of things, haven't I?" I asked.

"No," said Father. "You're right though, things have changed. I wouldn't worry too much about Walter. He'll recover in time. And in a few years, you'll meet a young man who will tell you he loves you, and you'll feel the same."

"Do you really think so?"

Father reached across the table and took my hand. "I'm certain of it." He squeezed and let go just as John pulled his boat up to the dock and shut off the motor.

"I can smell those burgers a mile off!" he said enthusiastically, climbing out onto the dock to join us. "Hope you saved me some fries."

Father slid a basket of them across the table. "Help yourself, John," he said. Then, as John dove in, Father turned to me and winked.

Chapter Twenty-Two

THE THRILL OF summer in Algonac had begun to wane as the late July temperatures rose and the Reid clan took to listless mornings and idle afternoons.

Hattie and John had headed home to Dearborn because it was "time to stop foolin' around and get back to work," as John had said, and things were more subdued without my cousins.

On a Saturday morning, though if truth be told it was nearly noon, Marigold tempted us all out of bed with a delicious breakfast of fried ham and eggs with buttermilk biscuits and blackberry jam.

"I can't remember the last time I ate anything so wonderful," I told Marigold, who beamed from the compliment.

"Put up that jam myself last summer, remember? You helped."

"I do remember," I said. "We should make some more this year. But this time, I'm taking enough jars to Cleveland to last the year."

Marigold laughed a hearty, happy laugh. "It's a date then. Maybe later today you could wash up the empty jars from the pantry. I'll go into town and see if I can't rustle up a bushel of berries."

With the promise of canning later in the day, I hurriedly cleared the table, though Marigold insisted *she* wash the dishes as Grandmother was dressed and pinning on her hat for her scheduled outing to the Algonac Cemetery to pay respects at Grandfather Reid's grave.

"You go on with Mrs. Reid," suggested Marigold. "We got plenty o' time for canning when you get back."

Soon Grandmother, Father, and I climbed into the Lincoln and rolled down the windows—the interior was as hot as an oven—and then headed into town. I did see some gray clouds clustering on the horizon. An omen of summer showers, perhaps, or a storm? Rain would be such a welcome respite from the heat.

The cemetery, surrounded by a tall iron fence, was located in the heart of Algonac, a sprawling lot planted with grass and young black oak trees. Algonac is proud of its black oaks and in fact is still home to the nation's largest, a National Champion Tree. In fact, Point du Chene, where the Reid's home was built, was given the French name which meant "Point of the Oaks" in English. When Grandfather passed away in 1922, Grandmother planted a sapling near his grave.

"Makes it easier to find," she told me as we ambled hand in hand across the grounds that sunny July morning. "Couldn't afford a headstone. Still can't. But no need. As long as this tree keeps growing, I'll always know where to find him."

The graveyard was dotted with waist-high granite markers, some dating back to the 1800s were covered with lichen and moss. Others were newer, still polished to a high shine, the names etched on them, bold against the gray stone. Dried Cottonwood leaves lay balanced on top of some of them, and a few more had been blown against their bases as the trees shed their spring leaves.

"The children were young when we moved here from Canada," said Grandmother. "Wasn't easy, leaving our family and home behind. Everything we'd known. But James insisted they'd have a good life here, and they have."

We reached the tree Grandmother had planted, which looked more like an unruly shrub these days, and Grandmother handed me the bouquet of daisies she'd cut from her garden. I took a few more steps to the spot I was certain of, since I'd visited here every year since I could remember, then bent and laid the flowers on the bare earth.

"Hat and John's baby is buried here, too," Grandmother reminded me. The baby boy had been stillborn and not given a name. The cemetery register listed him only as Witzig, his last name.

Behind me, I heard the click of Father's lighter. He didn't care for cemeteries. Though he never said so out loud, I could tell being among the dead made him feel uncomfortable. But he didn't let that stop him from accompanying his mother to his father's grave.

Decades later in the 1970s, when I visited Charles and Alice in Algonac before they retired and moved to Las Vegas, I came here again. By then, three additional members of the Reid family had been buried in this same plot, though there was only one very small pink granite headstone for Charles & Alice's little boy, Ross, who had drowned in 1955 just before his second birthday. The others included their baby girl, Margaret, stillborn in 1959, and Grandmother Reid, who passed away in 1944. But on that July morning in 1938, death felt far away. It was something that happened to those who grew old, who had lived their lives and had concluded them. Even the baby buried alongside Grandfather had no real place in my thoughts. That child had never taken a breath, never really lived at all, so death remained a distant, elusive thing that failed to coalesce into anything tangible in my mind.

Grandmother stood beside Grandfather's grave with her head reverently bowed, and her arms folded as if in prayer. The three of us said nothing but listened to the incessant chattering of the birds in the trees throughout the park. The peace was interrupted only by the muffled sound of a cough. I glanced up to see Father clutching a handkerchief to his mouth, the cigarette in his other hand forgotten as he coughed again and again into the cloth. For a moment, I worried he might not catch his breath, but then the coughing subsided, Father wiped his mouth dry, and tucked the handkerchief back into his pocket.

After a while, Grandmother let out a decisive breath before turning and taking Father's arm. "Thank you for coming with me, Bert. You know your father was so proud of you."

I could hear the smile in Father's voice as I followed behind them.

"I know, Mother. And I'm sure he's looking after you."

We continued through the wrought iron gate, and Father helped Grandmother back into the Lincoln. I climbed into the back seat, already dreaming of plump, fresh blackberries. As we drove away, I glanced back through the car window and tried to spot the oak that marked the Reid plot, but at this distance it looked just like all the other trees. I thought of Grandfather buried deep under the earth with no marker, no name to tell the world where he lay. Grandmother knew where to find him, but what would happen once she'd gone? Who would remain to remember him? Father, of course, and Aunt Hat and Father's other siblings. And me. I wasn't born yet when Grandfather passed, so I had no memories of him. But I knew of him from the stories Grandmother shared. James H. Reid had left a legacy behind. Surely a missing gravestone wouldn't matter. But still, it troubled me, and I couldn't help but wonder what happened to souls who lost their place in this world.

Turning back to face the front of the car, I vowed to remember, while in the distance, the clouds closed in.

Chapter Twenty-Three

WE WERE NEARLY packed. The time to leave Algonac grew nearer. Just one more day, and then we'd be leaving first thing in the morning. A sort of gloom had settled over the house as everyone anticipated the inevitable departure, everyone except Mother who had become almost militant about preparations.

After our last supper at Grandmother's, Mother and Alice chatted over the sink full of dirty dishes while Father and I lingered at the table, him reading the paper and me just being.

Suddenly, our silence was broken by Mother's voice.

"Bert, hand me that glass over there." Mother gestured impatiently at the tumbler just out of her reach on the kitchen counter. Father glanced up from the paper and let his gaze fall on Mother for just the briefest of moments before he folded the paper and set it aside. It was a look I'd seen countless times, an expression that said he did not wish to do her bidding but wouldn't cross the boundary they had between them by protesting.

Father rose from his chair and crossed the floor to the sink. I watched curiously as he curled his fingers around the half-empty glass and then hesitated just a moment before delivering it to Mother's outstretched hand. Through all this, she didn't look at him. Not once. As if she expected with absolute certainty that he would obey.

Looking back, I now understand that this was an event that had occurred probably thousands of times between them during the almost thirty years they had been married. Married people, over time, develop understandings, unspoken rules of what can and cannot be said and done, habits of restraint meant to avoid rocking the boat. Father was like that. Mother was a strong woman, rigid in her ways and often outspoken. Father, on the other hand, was cautious and reserved. Words to him were like a robin's egg, something to be handled with care.

Now at fourteen, I had been on the receiving end of mother's ire more times than I could count, and I could imagine Father had too in the early years before he learned to appease her. It's not that they didn't love each other. I'd seen them share pecks on the cheek and even hold hands plenty of times. But after three decades of marriage, I think they'd gotten comfortable with each other, or tired of each other.

In any case, Mother took the glass and set it in the tub of sudsy water, carrying on her conversation with Alice without pause. I expected Father to return to his paper, but instead he stood behind Mother for a few moments looking down at the top of her head.

"Dorothy," he said.

"But don't you know that the grocer had slipped in a bruised apple. Intentional, I tell you," Mother prattled on while Alice rocked little Gary in her arms.

"Dorothy," repeated Father in exactly the same tone as before, but Mother didn't seem to notice.

"So, I held up that apple and pointed to the brown spot on it, large as quarter, I tell you—"

"Dorothy."

Finally, Mother turned and for the first time all morning looked up into Father's face.

"What is it, Bertram?" she asked impatiently.

"I'm going down to the river for a spell."

Mother rinsed the glass in clean water and reached for a towel. "Well, I don't know why you'd trouble telling me." But then she paused and narrowed her eyes at him. "Are you feeling all right?" I was surprised by the honest concern in her voice, and by Father's expression, I guessed he was too.

He shook his head. "Just need some fresh air is all."

Mother didn't look completely satisfied, but she nodded anyway. "I'll send someone to fetch you for dinner later."

He kissed her cheek, and Mother's gaze lingered on him as he turned away, but then she returned to her conversation with Alice.

Father selected a cigarette from his case, took up the paper, and strolled out through the parlor to the porch, careful not to let the screen door slam shut behind him.

I followed him outside and kept my distance. He lit his cigarette as he strolled toward the river's edge and then just stood there for a while, gazing out over the water. At one point, he tipped his ashes into the ripples and watched them float away. Then he lowered himself to the grass, his knees bent in front of him, and opened the paper. Overhead, the clouds had darkened considerably.

I hesitated to approach. Father seemed quite contented in his solitude, but the serenity of the moment beckoned me.

"Daddy?" I asked, coming up beside him.

He squinted up at me through his spectacles. "Polka Dot," he said, smiling. "Has your mother called me back already? I was just about to read the Sports section."

"No, I just came to sit with you. If that's all right."

He patted the patch of grass beside him, and I sat down, tucking my skirt beneath my legs.

We sat quietly for a few minutes. It was late afternoon, and the sunlight from a stray break in the clouds sparkled like diamonds on the lazy rolling current.

"Hard to believe summer's come to an end for the Reid's," Father said. "I always feel a bit melancholy when it's time to leave Algonac."

"I do too," I said. "I wish we could stay here always."

Father laughed a little. "No, you don't. Winters are dreadful. I don't know how my mother and Marigold manage to survive it every year. Cleveland is cold enough as it is. I've often wondered what it would be like to winter somewhere warm, like Florida."

"Or California," I inserted. "Alberta says she loved it there."

Father drew from his cigarette and let the smoke curl out from his lips. "I admit I envy Alberta. It was daring of her to live there. Quite the adventurer."

"She told me once she hopes to go back one day, but right now she likes being close to home, close to you and Mother."

"Chicago isn't close enough, I'm afraid." Father closed his eyes and rubbed his forehead with the pad of his thumb. "Family should be together. Nothing's more essential than family, even good weather."

He opened his eyes and grinned at me. Then Father folded his paper and wrapped an arm around my shoulders. "So, have you heard from Walter in the past few days?"

I glided my palm across the blades of grass. "No," I said.

"Have you called on him?"

"No. Honestly, I wouldn't know what to say. It was all so awkward."

Overhead, a flock of ducks flew by in V formation. They were so majestic as they passed. I wondered if they were already leaving Algonac too.

Father gave me a gentle squeeze. "I think Walter would be disappointed if you didn't say goodbye, don't you?"

It was true. I was sure Walter would want me to say goodbye. I'd imagined standing at his porch and rapping on his door dozens of times, but I could never say the right thing.

"I'd only make things worse," I said.

Father thoughtfully examined his cigarette, now no more than a stub, and then tossed it into the river. It floated for a while like a little boat, then sunk beneath the surface.

"It's your call, Polka Dot."

All of a sudden, I felt a drop of water plunk onto the tip of my nose. Father held out his palm where several more raindrops landed. He got to his feet and brushed the grass and soil from the back of his trousers. Then he took my hand and helped me up. "I suppose we'd better finish packing our things and help your grandmother clean up the house. By this time tomorrow, we'll be home."

Home. Sometimes, though, Algonac felt more like home than home did. I think Father felt the same. That's probably why he lingered on the riverbank that day, even after I'd gone back to the house. Over the years, I've spent a lot of time remembering that image of him, standing there in the rain, hands in his pockets, silhouetted against the glistening water, and I've often wondered if he somehow knew it was the last time he'd see his beloved St. Clair.

We were all packed, and Grandmother's house was spic and span by bedtime. In the morning, we all woke early and enjoyed a feast of ham and eggs and toast with jam that Marigold had prepared for the occasion. Afterwards, Aunt Florence came by to wish us well.

"Won't be quite the same around here without you all," she said, distributing hugs all around. She paused when she reached Alice.

"Chic picked himself a good one," Florence said, giving her an especially warm embrace. "You take good care of yourself and that little boy of yours." Florence stepped back and cut a look at Charles. "You two belong here. I just feel it in my marrow."

Charles laughed and slid his arm around Alice's waist, but Alice seemed to take Florence's words more seriously. "Thank you, Florence," she said and returned Aunt Florence's embrace.

Next, it was Marigold's turn to say her goodbyes. "I'm gonna miss you, Dottie," she said to me, wiping her eyes with the corner of her apron. "You come on back next year. Y'hear me?"

I gave Marigold the biggest hug I could muster. Then I did the same for Grandmother.

"Thank you for letting us stay," I told her.

Grandmother beamed at me. "That attic room is yours whenever you want it, Dorothy Ann. Marigold'll keep it ready. Won't you, Marigold?"

Marigold started a new wave of tears. Father hugged her and dabbed her eyes with his handkerchief. "You and Mother look after each other," he said. "Call me should anything happen. You got plenty of stores for winter?"

"We shore do," Marigold said.

"Plenty of firewood?"

Grandmother clucked impatiently. "You know we do. You cut most of it yourself. Now, you all should get a move on. Storm's only getting fiercer."

Father wrapped his arms around Grandmother, and they held each other for a long time. When they finally parted, Grandmother's eyes were wet with tears.

"I love you, Mother," Father said.

"Go on now," Grandmother said in reply. "Time's a wasting."

Mother, Charles, and Alice all said their farewells, and then Grandmother kissed baby Gary and gave his pudgy fist a little squeeze. Finally, we all dashed out into the rain, clambered into the Lincoln, and set off.

As we drove away, I thought of Walter. I never did say goodbye to him. I just couldn't bring myself to do it, and I was already regretting it. But it was too late to turn back now. I could always write him a letter. And besides, I reasoned, there would always be next summer.

Dorthy Ann Reid – Circa 1941

Reid Family, circa 1900
Front Row: James Reid & Margaret Sommerville Reid
Middle Row: (order unknown) Florence, Harriet & Ethel
Back Row: (order unknown) Herbert, Harry & Gordon
Bertram Reid is in back row on the right

Bertram Wallace Reid & Dorothy May (Noble) Reid,
circa 1930s

Bertram Reid in the Cleveland Union Club,
circa 1930's

Dorothy May Reid holding Dorothy Ann Reid,
circa 1926

Dorothy May & Dorothy Ann Reid
@ Dorothy Ann's high school graduation, circa 1942

Chic (Charles) & Larry (Alice) Reid, circa 1936

Clara Petronella Peabody Noble
(Grandma Pratt), circa 1940

Part Two:
Cleveland – 1938 to 1939

Chapter Twenty-Four

In the fall of 1938, the world was changing in many ways. In Germany, Adolf Hitler and Joseph Goebbels ignited a night of violence in Germany, destroying 7500 businesses and synagogues, and killing 91 Jews. It would later come to be known as Kristallnacht.

Elsewhere, electroshock therapy was introduced, the first xerographs were printed, and the ballpoint pen was invented.

And in the United States, the Fair Labor Standards Act went into effect, setting the nation's first minimum wage at 25 cents an hour. Unemployment was 19%, a gallon of gasoline was 20 cents, and the cost of a postage stamp was 3 cents.

Dramatic changes in history don't always happen in spectacular ways, like a bomb detonating or an unexpected earthquake. Most occur gradually, over time. Often the gradations of change are so subtle that their significance remains undetected until it all culminates in a single climactic moment where the world seemingly topples off its axis. Once that happens, nothing is ever the same again.

We arrived home just before two o'clock. Father dropped off Charles, Alice, and baby Gary at their place first, then he delivered me and Mother at our front door before pulling into the driveway to unload the luggage.

As I stepped up to the porch, the door swung open, and Sadie was there to greet us with open arms. Even Mother accepted a hug from her.

"Welcome home, Mrs. Reid, Dorothy Ann. Someone's been waitin' for you." I stepped inside, and Knickers, my cat, immediately started caressing my ankles, walking around me in circles and brushing her coat and tail against my shoes and stockings. I eagerly gathered her into my arms.

"Oh Knickers! How I've missed you!"

While Sadie brought Mother up to speed on how she'd looked after the house in our absence and filled her in on the news around town, I headed to the side door to help Father. He'd already set most of the bags on the step.

"Can I help?" I asked.

Father used his index finger to adjust his spectacles. "Why don't you carry your mother's trunk into the hall," he said with a laugh, knowing full well it was far too heavy for me. "I'm teasing, Polka Dot. Just take your bag, if you don't mind. Take it right up to your room and unpack, or your mother will soon be on both our cases."

I did as I was told, grasping the handle of my carpet bag with one hand and cradling Knickers with the other. Entering my room, I felt a wash of relief. I dropped the bag to the floor and let myself fall back onto my bed. Sadie had kept it neat and tidy, probably dusted every day, knowing her. And how I appreciated it.

It felt so good to be home.

Later, Sadie served us a delicious welcome home dinner of meatloaf and mashed potatoes, Father's favorite, followed by her famous banana pudding and whipped cream. By the time we'd finished eating, I was stuffed to the brim and feeling quite drowsy.

After supper, Mother and Father retired to the sitting room, Mother to work on her knitting and Father to drink his evening coffee and listen to the wireless. How easily they settled back into their usual routines, I thought. Summer in Algonac had been one, long adventure. But here, back home in Cleveland, the adventure was over, and everything seemed back to normal. Suddenly, seeing my parents sitting together but absorbed in their own little worlds, I missed Algonac more than ever before.

After helping Sadie with the dishes, I went to the sitting room to say goodnight. I gave Mother a quick kiss on the cheek.

"What are you making?" I asked, indicating the baby blue yarn twitching between her needles.

"Never you mind," she said with a guarded smile. "I've been waiting all summer to start this project. You go on to bed now."

Father set his coffee cup on the lamp table and reached his arms out to me. I went to him and sat in his lap as he enfolded those strong arms around me. I hadn't done that since before we'd left on vacation.

"It's been a good summer, hasn't it, Polka Dot?"

"It has," I said, laying my head against his shoulder. I loved the smell of him, the ever-present aroma of quality tobacco and the peppermints he kept in a tin in his breast pocket. "Maybe the best summer ever."

"You say that every year," said Mother with a little laugh.

"And that's the way it should be," said Father. "Make sure you file away the memories, like a photograph album in your heart. That way when things here at home are not as exciting as you'd like them to be, you can go back and visit Algonac anytime you like. Isn't that so, Dorothy?"

Mother shrugged and continued knitting, squinting her eyes at the stitches.

"Just you remember what I said," Father continued, giving me a knowing look. "It's best to remember the happiest of times and let the hurtful or disappointing ones go. Does no good to hold onto the past if it brings us pain."

I recalled our talk at Sid's just a few days earlier about Walter and wondered if that's what he meant.

I kissed Father's cheek and said goodnight to him, then I headed for my room. I took my time changing into my nightgown, trying to drag out the day as long as possible. That morning, I'd been in Algonac. I'd said goodbye to the river, to the trees, to my grandmother and Marigold. But I hadn't said goodbye to Walter. I felt guilty about it, but I hadn't been ready to face him after the way I'd treated him at Tashmoo Park.

I climbed into my bed and wondered if I'd done the right thing. I really didn't know. And now that I was home in Cleveland, it was too late to change things anyway. Best to move forward, I told myself. Like Father said. No sense holding onto the past. I would write to Walter and apologize, I determined, and soon.

Then I reached for the chain on my lamp and tugged on it. The light switched off, and soon I was fast asleep.

Chapter Twenty-Five

THE WEEKS BETWEEN coming home from Algonac and the first day of school passed like a whirlwind. Mother took me shopping for a new school bag and fabric for my dresses, which she and Sadie sewed with expertise. By Labor Day, I had a complete wardrobe. I found the fittings dull, but I loved the rich textures and colors of the blouses and skirts that now hung in my closet and was anxious to show them off.

"You might want to wear this your first day back, though it's your decision," Mother said, holding up a blue and gray plaid jumper with wide, neatly pressed pleats and covered buttons. As I modeled it in the full-length mirror, Knickers batted playfully at the hem with her paw.

Next, Mother presented me with a light blue knitted poncho to match.

"So that's what you were being so secretive about," I teased. It was soft as a kitten and just as warm.

"It's for when the weather turns," Mother said, adjusting it over my shoulders proudly. "Too warm to wear now, but in the winter…"

"It's perfect!" I said with enthusiasm. "Thank you."

I kissed Mother as she folded the poncho and laid it neatly on my bed. After she left the room, I again tried on each of my new outfits, trying to decide which to wear on my first day of school. I finally settled on Mother's suggested jumper.

"Perfect," I said again, wondering if Judy and Betty's outfits could ever compare. But on that first Monday back, my friends were dressed in equally impressive new outfits as well, and we fawned over each other.

"It's so good to see you, Dottie!" said Judy, greeting me with an excited squeeze. "Summer was so long and boring without you."

Judy was a natural beauty with ebony hair and eyes, and porcelain skin. She was the envy of every girl at school. We'd known each other most of our lives, both our families having attended the same church for as long as I could remember.

"Summer's always long and boring without Dot," replied Betty with a wink. "Can't we keep you just once? You missed all the excitement."

Betty had made us a threesome in sixth grade when she'd moved to Cleveland from Detroit. We'd all been inseparable ever since. I had to admit that I did miss my friends each summer, but I couldn't imagine anything more fun in Cleveland than what I experienced in Algonac: the fishing, the boating, Tashmoo Park, and of course, Walter.

"What happened?" I asked, shifting my nearly empty book bag to my other shoulder. By the end of the day, it would be weighed down with textbooks.

Judy took my hand and led me to a bench where the three of us sat down. "Well, for one thing, Billy Brown asked Betty to the Independence Day dance!"

Betty, silent beside her, blushed.

"Did you go?" I asked, hoping to coax her out of her shell. Of the three of us, she was the quietest and least likely to brag.

She nodded. "I had a grand time," she said. "I wish you were there."

146

"I went with Patrick Dewey," said Judy. "You remember him, don't you? He was in our history class last year. Red hair? Freckles? He's rather nice, actually, and turns out he's a keen dancer."

"But," said Betty coyly, "we want to hear about Walter."

"Oh yes," said Judy. "The few letters you sent were so cryptic. Walter and I did this. Walter and I did that. Well?"

Fortunately, the first bell rang, warning us that we had just a few minutes to get to our classes. We'd already attended orientation where we received our schedules. I was disappointed that I shared only two classes with Judy and one with Betty. We had no classes with all of us together, though we pledged to eat lunch together every day. High school would be a different experience for all of us, but I looked forward to the adventure.

For now, I was grateful not to have to explain how complicated things had become between Walter and I. Like Judy, he'd been a life-long friend, but the world in which we existed was completely separate from here in Cleveland. I wasn't sure how I felt about those two worlds coming in contact with each other.

By the time I made it home from school, I was exhausted but eager to dive into my first day's assignments. Mother had always insisted I do my homework right after school and before dinner, leaving my evenings free to be with the family.

Since it was only day one, the requirements were light, and I'd finished my Algebra page and reading assignments with plenty of time to spare. So, I decided to slip into the kitchen to help Sadie prepare dinner. I was surprised to find Father standing at the sink instead of Sadie.

"You're home early," I said, hugging him from behind. He wore Mother's frilled apron over his slacks, dress shirt, and tie. His sleeves were rolled up, and his arms were wet up to the elbows washing dishes. I noticed a few droplets of water on his spectacles as well.

He patted my hands with a damp, sudsy palm. "The shop was

147

slow this afternoon, and I was feeling a bit under the weather. So, I closed up."

"And Mother put you right to work, I see."

He glanced at me with a conspiratorial smile. "Actually, she doesn't know. She thinks I'm napping on the couch."

He chuckled, but it suddenly transformed into a cough. The sound of it came from deep in his chest. I recalled how bad it had sounded at the cemetery in Algonac, and how he'd blamed it on allergies. Now, he quickly dried his hands on a dish towel and held a fist to his mouth. But in a few seconds, the coughing had subsided.

"That's not allergies. You've caught a cold," I suggested. "Maybe you *should* be napping."

Father again smiled. "I'd rather be shooting the breeze with you." He dipped his hand into the sink and then flicked some suds at me. We both laughed.

"Just promise me you'll rest," I told him.

"I promise," he said.

Then I went in search of Sadie, looking for instructions on what to prepare for supper. The plan was rosemary roasted chicken with mashed potatoes and collard greens. The potatoes needed peeling and boiling, something I was happy to do.

Father had gone by the time I returned to the kitchen. The sink was empty of water, and the dishes had been dried and put away in the cupboard. I gathered half a dozen potatoes from the root bin and carefully sliced away the skins. Then I rinsed them and put them in a pot of water on the stove to boil.

I thought about Father and that nasty cough he'd brought home from work. I wondered if we had any Cepacol drops in the house. Curious as to where he'd gone, I snuck quietly to the kitchen door and pushed it open. Peaking around it into the sitting room, I spotted Father lying on the sofa, eyes closed, an afghan pulled to his chin.

Chapter Twenty-Six

IT HAD BEEN more than a month since I'd last seen Walter, and I had spent nearly every day thinking about our day at Tashmoo Park, the warmth of my hand in his, how I'd felt so safe and comfortable with him, and how suddenly everything went off kilter when he told me he cared more for me than just a friend. The truth was, I may have felt the same way, but it just seemed wrong somehow.

The first Friday after school, I couldn't concentrate on homework. My mind kept drifting back to the memories I'd accumulated of me and Walter over the years: fishing off the pier, sunning ourselves after swimming in the river, getting wet and sticky eating watermelon at the festival. Our friendship meant the world to me, and I couldn't bear the thought of it coming to an end the way it had.

So, I pushed aside my schoolbooks and laid out a sheet of the stationery Walter had given me. Clutching a sharpened pencil in my right hand, I hovered over the blank page, wondering what to write.

"Dear Walter…"

I carefully sketched the words on the paper, but that was as far as I could go. After that, my mind went numb. I rolled some possible ideas around in my mind:

I'm sorry about what happened that day at Tashmoo. The truth was, I wasn't prepared to hear—

Let's forget the whole thing and be friends. No sense letting—

Please forgive my childish response. I didn't mean to hurt your feelings—

But nothing sounded quite right.

I must have sat there for half an hour, pondering which words might adequately express how I felt before I realized that none of them did my feelings justice because I couldn't even pin down those feelings. I was as flabbergasted now as I was the moment it all happened. I just couldn't organize my thoughts into words.

I spread my fingers and lay my palm against the page, then I made a fist, crumpling the blank letter in my hand, and tossed it into the wastebasket. I wasn't ready to write to Walter, not yet at least. I'd give myself a little more time to think and then try again in a few days.

I reached for my world history textbook and opened the cover, forcing myself to focus. It didn't take long before I was absorbed, and by the time I'd finished reading the chapter on Mesopotamia, and had begun writing my summary due in class on Monday, Walter had been pushed to a far corner of my mind.

Over the weekend, Judy and I made arrangements to get together to discuss the book we were reading in Literature class. We had agreed to read the assigned chapters on our own and then meet for lunch on Saturday. Sadie prepared the perfect picnic for us: ham and cheese sandwiches, fruit salad, and fresh-baked chocolate chip cookies. We spread out a blanket at the park and enjoyed our food and the coolness of the day. Despite occasional rain showers, September was still warm, but there was a tinge of autumn in the air, heralding a change in the weather.

After we exhausted our impressions of the book, we lay back in the shade of a tree and closed our eyes, letting the breeze drift over us.

"You going to the dance next weekend?" Judy asked after a while. I'd seen the leaflet being distributed around school. A back-to-school dance and celebration.

"I hadn't really thought about it," I told her. "Are you going?"

"Of course, I am. Who isn't?" Judy propped her head on her elbow. "Betty says her brother Jim will drive us and take us home. We could even stop for milk shakes after. Wouldn't that be fun?"

I listened to her as she went on and on about why I had to go to the party, and after a while, she convinced me. However, Mother was not prone to giving her consent for things as frivolous as parties, especially for "girls my age". I was now fourteen, and as Mother had reminded me on at least one previous occasion, my sister Alberta had not attended her first soiree until fifteen. But what did I have to lose by asking?

I told Judy I'd let her know. We finished up our homework, and Judy headed home for supper.

I was quieter than usual at the dinner table that night, my mind whirling with thoughts about how to approach the subject, but Father did it for me.

"You seem lost in thought," he said as Sadie set out slices of apple pie for dessert. "You've hardly said a word. What's on your mind, Polka Dot?"

Mother lifted her eyes to me, now expectant.

"Yes," I said hesitantly. I fiddled with the spoon beside my plate. Father took a bite of his pie. "Judy was over today."

"I saw her," said Father. "She's grown taller since I last saw her.

Quite the young lady, wouldn't you say, Dorothy?"

Mother nodded disinterestedly.

"Well, Judy invited me to a party next weekend, a dance. Most of the kids at school will be going."

Mother's fork froze halfway to her mouth. "I have a hard time believing Judy's mother would allow her to attend. She's only thirteen."

"She just turned fourteen," I replied.

Mother *hurumphed* and ate her dessert. "Still awfully young for mingling with boys at a party unsupervised."

"It will be supervised. Several of the teachers and administration will be there. It's going to be in the school gymnasium. I'd really like to go."

Mother finished off her pie, then stood and carried her plate to the sink. "A girl your age should be focused on her studies, not on gallivanting around. Now, finish your dessert. Sadie's gone home for the night, so I'd appreciate some help washing up."

I looked at Father who was quietly scraping his fork against his plate. I hoped he'd speak up for me, but it appeared as though he and Mother were in harmony. I would have to let Judy know that she and Betty would be going without me.

Chapter Twenty-Seven

THE NEXT FEW days passed quickly, and once I'd let Judy know I couldn't go to the party, I'd forgotten all about it. At least I did my best to forget about it. I buried myself in homework and spent my evenings reading assignments for the next day. At night, I'd climb under my blankets and listen to my father coughing downstairs. He'd been spending more and more time sleeping on the couch, presumably to avoid keeping Mother awake. One night, I asked him about seeing a doctor. He said he already had, several times, but that it was nothing I should worry about. He smiled, kissed my forehead, and wished me peaceful dreams. But his words didn't ease my mind, nor did the hours I'd lay awake concerned about his coughing which continued long after I'd finally fall asleep.

Friday at school, I had to listen to Judy and Betty and a lot of other kids chitter away excitedly about the party Saturday night. I pretended that I didn't care, that I was happy for them. I even lied and said I had other plans, which I didn't, beyond eating dinner with my family and studying, as usual.

Despite my best efforts to stay positive, the fact was I was feeling rather dismal by the time I came home. To my surprise, Father had taken off work early and was in the living room reading the day's newspaper.

"You're home early again," I said, greeting him with a kiss.

He folded his paper and removed his spectacles, setting them on the lamp table. "I am. Worn out."

"Well, you haven't been sleeping well. No wonder you're tired."

He nodded in agreement. His expression seemed weary, but he smiled for me anyway.

"I've actually been waiting for you," he said, a mischievous glint appearing in his eye. "About that party at the school—"

I interrupted him. "It's not a big deal," I lied. "I've forgotten all about it."

He studied me for a moment, and I could see that he knew I was hiding the truth. But he didn't call me out.

"I know how much you want to go, but I have to agree with your mother. You're a little young for such gatherings."

My heart sank. For a moment, I'd thought maybe he might have changed his mind, or at least offered to talk to Mother about it.

Father seemed to sense my disappointment. He tucked a gentle finger under my chin. "Chin up," he said, a peculiar look passing behind his eyes. "There's always next year. In the meantime," he continued, "I have a proposal."

Father reached for something on the table, something he'd set his glasses on. He slid out a pair of rectangular pieces of stiff paper and held them up for me to see. My eyes widened, and I gasped.

"Those are tickets to an Indians game!"

"They're not the greatest seats," said Father, "but they're for tomorrow night's game at League Park. One of the last of the season."

I couldn't believe it. Father wasn't much for baseball, or any sport for that matter. I'd gone to one game with him years before, but I'd been so young I didn't remember much about it except that we left early because I was bored and sleepy.

"I took you to a game once," Father said as if reading my mind.

154

"But you were too young to appreciate it. I used to take Chic and Bertie every so often, but I haven't been in years. If you're not interested—"

He feigned putting the tickets away, but before he could, I threw my arms around his neck and pressed my cheek against his. His skin was rough with afternoon whiskers but warm.

"I'd love to go," I whispered into him. "This is better than any old party could ever be."

He patted my shoulder, and as I pulled away I saw his eyes were moist with tears, which he quickly swiped away with his handkerchief.

"Well, good," he said. "It's a date."

The Cleveland Stadium was the largest Major Baseball League stadium in the country, seating more than 78,000 fans, and had been the official home of the Cleveland Indians since it's construction in 1931. Charles had described the games he'd attended in detail, and I'd always thought it would be fun to go once I was older. But then he got married and was busy with his new job and little Gary, so I didn't dare ask him to take me. I had never expected Father would be the one to do it.

But sometimes, games were still held at the much smaller League Park, seating only 4,000, which would eventually be demolished in 1951. Father's tickets were for a game scheduled there, but I didn't mind one bit. A baseball game in any venue would be nothing short of sensational!

The parking lot was already filling with cars by the time we arrived with just fifteen minutes to spare before the game was to begin against the Detroit Tigers. As Father and I made our way through the crush of fans to find our seats, we both couldn't help but grin and laugh.

The game got underway with the Tigers first up to bat. Though one of their players made it to first base, three others struck out before he could get any farther. This was good news to us, of course, and the audience cheered as the first Indians player, Tommy Irwin, came up to bat. He walked to first base, as did the next player, Roy Weatherly. After Averill struck out, Jeff Heath walked, which meant Irwin was on third and Weatherly on second. When a player named Trosky hit a fly ball, Irwin ran for home and scored the game's first run.

The truth was I wasn't very familiar with the team or much about baseball at all. So, Father narrated every play for me, giving me the names of the men at bat, and soon I knew them all. Later in life, I came to really love baseball and was a loyal fan of the Anaheim Angels in California. Though I couldn't afford to attend games in person often, I listened on the radio and eventually watched games on television. But on October 1, 1938, my first true exposure to baseball, I felt like it was a completely new world, and I was enthralled. I studied how each man strolled to the plate, how he'd adjust his grip along the bat's handle, how his focus would narrow to a penetrating point aimed at the pitcher. I loved the shape of the pitcher's back as he pressed the ball into his glove and glanced at the bases before swinging his arm back and letting the ball fly. The speed of the ball defied imagination. Sometimes the only way I knew it had flown was when I heard the thud of it in the catcher's mitt or the resounding *thwack* as the wooden bat connected with it. The whole experience was simply thrilling.

By end of the seventh inning, the Tigers had scored no runs, while the Indians had scored five, three of them at the bottom of the sixth inning. I'd screamed so much my voice had gone hoarse, but I didn't care. It was all so exciting. The seventh and eighth innings moved quickly, with lots of outs and no runs for either team. I noticed, as Detroit came to bat at the top of the ninth, that every nerve was taut and my heart was beating fast and hard. They stood little chance of winning or even tying the game at this point, but still, one never knew what could happen. Father grew tensely silent as the first player, a fellow named McCoy, hit the ball to center field and got on first base. The next player doubled, moving McCoy to third, setting him up for an easy run. I felt my heart sink when McCoy stepped onto third base, leaning in toward home, ready for the dash.

Next, a player by the name of Cullenbine struck out, followed by a second strike out by Greenberg. Two strikes for the Tigers. The anticipation was almost more than I could bear.

As York stepped up to bat, Father cocked his head at me, an amused grin on his face. "You're biting your nails," he pointed out. And I was, though I hadn't realized it. Mother wouldn't approve if she knew, so I dutifully clasped my hands in my lap. The pitcher peered at York from beneath the brim of his cap. He gave a little nod and then let the ball fly. I heard the dull *thwop* of it against the catcher's leather mitt. Strike one. The catcher took his time throwing the ball back to the pitcher, who surveyed the two players on base. Just as he was about to throw again, McCoy made his move, or at least tried. He started for home, but the pitcher saw it and threw the ball to third base. McCoy returned just in time, his attempt to steal home failed.

The pitcher released the ball, and York swung — and missed! Strike two! It looked like McCoy might make one more attempt for home, and as the pitcher threw the ball one last time, he took off for it. But York swung and missed again. Strike three!

The crowd around me erupted in a deafening roar. Thousands got to their feet, shouting and applauding. I looked at Father who leaned back in his chair, a pleased look on his face.

"What now?" I asked.

He shrugged. "Game's over. We won."

"We won?"

"We won."

As the crowds around us massed toward the exits, Father and I remained in our seats. We finished off the Cracker Jacks we'd bought during the fifth inning, reveling in victory. It wasn't until the stadium had nearly emptied before we got up and headed for our car. We were silent as we walked, though I was bursting with excitement and could have said a hundred things. But that wasn't Father's way. I wanted to know what he was thinking, wanted to discuss some of the more interesting moments of the game, but instead I reached for his hand. He curled his fingers around mine, and somehow, as if words had lost their need for meaning, Father and I communicated more clearly than we ever had before, and never would again.

Chapter Twenty-Eight

THE INDIANS PLAYED a second game against the Tigers that weekend and lost 4 to 1. So, Father and I had lucked out to see them beat Detroit first. We decided to not let the news of the subsequent loss spoil our victory. For years to come, I would look back at that game with great affection, and it would endear me to the sport long after I'd left Cleveland behind.

The next few weeks passed in a whirlwind of school assignments and plans for Halloween. I was to accompany Judy in taking her younger brother and sister out trick-or-treating. Though I considered myself too old for it now, I still wanted to dress up to keep in the spirit of things.

Halloween fell on a Monday, which meant Sunday was a flurry of last minute repairs to my clown costume and doing a run-through with my face make-up. I certainly didn't want to frighten Judy's siblings, so I decided to keep it to a minimum: a red nose, a wide happy smile, and rosy cheeks. Mother had purchased the paints and a brush from a local shop along with a wig of poofy blue hair. She'd sewn the costume herself two years earlier, but it was baggy enough to still fit, though the legs now fell several inches above my ankles, which actually added to the comical nature of the ensemble.

Sunday night on the 30th, I wanted to do a run-though to see how everything would look. I finished the make-up and had just donned the costume, but I needed some help with the wig, so I made my way to the sitting room where Father and Mother were listening to the wireless' "Mercury Theater on the Air" before retiring to bed.

"Mother, could you help—" I began as I entered the room.

Mother responded with an abrupt "Shhhh!" She was sitting in her favorite chair but leaning forward, her knitting paused in her lap, intently listening to the program. Father looked a bit more relaxed, his eyes closed, his fingers splayed across the armrest. They were clearly engrossed in the program. Curious, I paused to listen.

"Ladies and gentlemen, here is the latest bulletin from the Intercontinental Radio News. Toronto, Canada: Professor Morse of McMillan University reports observing a total of three explosions on the planet Mars, between the hours of 7:45 P. M. and 9:20 P. M., eastern standard time. This confirms earlier reports received from American observatories. Now, nearer home, comes a special bulletin from Trenton, New Jersey. It is reported that at 8:50 P. M. a huge, flaming object, believed to be a meteorite, fell on a farm in the neighborhood of Grovers Mill, New Jersey, twenty-two miles from Trenton. The flash in the sky was visible within a radius of several hundred miles and the noise of the impact was heard as far north as Elizabeth. We have dispatched a special mobile unit to the scene, and will have our commentator, Carl Phillips, give you a word picture of the scene as soon as he can reach there from Princeton. In the meantime, we take you to the Hotel Martinet in Brooklyn, where Bobby Millette and his orchestra are offering a program of dance music."

The announcer stopped speaking and music began to play, but soon another announcer cut through:

"Ladies and gentlemen, this is Carl Phillips again, out of the Wilmuth farm, Grovers Mill, New Jersey. Professor Pierson and myself made the eleven miles from Princeton in ten minutes. Well,

I... hardly know where to begin, to paint for you a word picture of the strange scene before my eyes, like something out of a modern 'Arabian Nights.' Well, I just got here. I haven't had a chance to look around yet. I guess that's it. Yes, I guess that's the thing, directly in front of me, half buried in a vast pit. Must have struck with terrific force. The ground is covered with splinters of a tree it must have struck on its way down. What I can see of the object itself doesn't look very much like a meteor, at least not the meteors I've seen. It looks more like a huge cylinder. It has a diameter of... what would you say, Professor Pierson?"

I took a seat on the sofa, the wig all but forgotten. What was this strange cylinder they were talking about? I had to know. As the news story went on, it became evident that they were talking about an invasion. Earth had been invaded by Martians! My chest tightened, and breathing became a trial. This couldn't be happening, could it? I looked to my parents for confirmation, but though Mother gripped her knitting needles with a white-knuckle tenacity, there was no fear on her face but an almost pleasurable interest. Father was as calm as ever, leaning back in his chair, eyes still closed as if nearly asleep.

Finally, I couldn't bear it anymore.

"Mother," I asked in as quiet a whisper as I could muster, "what's going on?"

She cut me an irritated glance and gave a sharp sigh. "It's a broadcast, a radio play of that novel *War of the Worlds*. Now, let me get back to it. I'm just dying to know what happens next."

A radio play. A story! The tight knot in my stomach relented, and I laid back against the cushions to listen. I had to admit, it was very convincing. I'd come in after the opening where the announcer had introduced the story and the players. Later, I would learn that other people misinterpreted the broadcast as a report of a real space invasion as well, but the rumors that there was mass panic and people killed themselves rather than be taken hostage by the Martians

161

became a bigger story than Welles' performance itself.

The next day, I asked Judy about it, but she hadn't heard the broadcast at all, didn't even know what I was talking about. So, we took her siblings trick-or-treating as planned and I didn't mention it again.

It was several weeks later when Father brought it up after dinner one night. He'd been reading the paper.

"Germany annexed Sudetenland a couple months ago. Before that, they annexed Austria. Do you know what annex means, Polka Dot?"

I said I didn't.

"It's a pleasant way of saying invasion. Germany has taken control of those countries and will likely do the same to others."

We sat with our soiled plates still in front of us. Mother had taken hers to the sink and had retired to the living room to continue her knitting. She normally didn't approve of Father reading the paper at the table, but the serious expression on his face suggested that there was something on his mind. He folded the paper and laid it beside his plate. Then he turned his eyes on me.

"No one wants to be invaded, annexed, whatever people in power might call it. It goes against the drive for freedom God gave us humans. And it's in our nature to fight back."

My mind flashed back to the night we listened to *War of the Worlds*, how creatures from another planet had attempted to take possession of Earth, and how the people fought back. I thought to myself that Father must be connecting the story of the Martians to the Nazi Party controlling Germany. But as far as I knew, Austria hadn't fought against Germany. They seemed to have welcomed them in.

"Sometimes," Father continued, "the enemy invades so slowly that the host doesn't even know it at first. It's tentacles spread through ignorance and apathy. That's what's happening in Europe.

But it won't take long for someone to wake up, to say enough is enough."

"Do you think there will be a war?" I asked.

His gaze drifted away for a moment, as if his mind had shifted gears. "Invasion. War. It's not just about nations," he said almost dreamily. "They are just as real inside ourselves."

Inside ourselves? What was he talking about? The distance between us grew suddenly wider, and I felt the urge to draw him back. "Well," I said, "the Martians were defeated not by guns but by a disease, weren't they? Maybe the Germans will be defeated like that, not from a cold, of course, but by their own frailty within."

"I'd like to think that," Father replied. He stood up and collected both our plates, the utensils rattling against the glass. Just as he set them in the sink, a sudden coughing fit overtook him. His chest heaved for breath for nearly a minute before he finally got hold of himself. "Talk about a cold," he said with an ironic laugh. Then he turned his gaze out the window. "It's all well and good to fight an enemy and hope for victory, but what should one do if defeat is inevitable?"

The question was not directed at me. In fact, I was certain he'd forgotten I was there at all. When he removed his spectacles to rub his eyes, I was sure of it. Because he turned his back to me and left the room without even saying goodnight. I glanced at the paper he'd been reading and saw there was nothing about Germany on the page.

Chapter Twenty-Nine

THANKSGIVING CAME AND went so quickly I hardly had time to enjoy it. Alice and Charles hosted at their home for the first time. Father dropped me off early in the morning to help. While Charles prepared the turkey (wearing Alice's apron to boot), she and I peeled and boiled potatoes, peeled and baked the yams, diced bread for the stuffing, and kneaded dough for the rolls. Mother and Sadie were back at home making pecan and pumpkin pies, which they would bring over later.

Once the preparations were done, and the turkey was in the oven, we turned our attention to cleaning so the house would be at its tip top finest when the guests arrived, which included Mother and Father, as well as Alice's parents. Soon the house shone like newly polished silver, and the air smelled of rosemary and thyme.

The dinner itself was simply grand, with a loud bustle of happy voices and the clinking of utensils against Alice's best china. Everyone ate their fill, even little Gary who, now at six months, adored mashed potatoes. The food was devoured all too soon and the plates cleared. Pie would come later after we'd had time to digest a bit. Father and Charles washed the dishes and put them away, a nice change from the usual routine, while Alice gave Gary his nightly bath and put him down for bed. The entire day was a rush of joy and gratitude, ending with a slur of kisses and embraces. When I got home late that night, I didn't even remember climbing into bed. I fell asleep before my head hit the pillow.

With Thanksgiving behind us, Mother immediately switched her focus toward Christmas.

"Alberta and Harold will be coming," she explained, studying our first flurry of snow outside the living room window as she buttoned up her overcoat. "So, I want a spruce fir. Your father always chooses the nicest trees."

Father had left for work early that morning, so I hadn't even had a chance to kiss him goodbye. When I asked Mother about it, she simply shrugged. "Left nearly two hours early," she said. "Must've had some errands to run. It is Christmas," she added with a sly smile. "Who knows what devious plans he's got up his sleeve this year."

Father was known for surprises. One year, he'd been secretive for months only to surprise Mother on Christmas day with a new Hoover vacuum. And it had been just two years ago he'd surprised her with the Lincoln.

"I think I'll buy him a new scarf," I suggested. Mother paused and looked at me curiously. "He can't seem to shake that cold he's had. He should stay extra warm this winter."

Mother nodded in agreement. "It does seem to come and go. I suggested he see a doctor about it."

"What did he say?"

"He insisted he was fine. But a scarf would be nice. Don't want him coming down with pneumonia. I'll help you pick one out at Sears & Roebuck."

I'd already been scouring its catalog for one, but I was certain I'd want to choose it in person from the store, so I appreciated Mother's offer.

Later that day in school, a scarf for Father was about all I could think of. Betty poked me during English class when I failed to respond to the teacher's question. Thankfully, I woke from my reverie quick enough for him not to notice. "Thanks," I whispered to Betty afterwards.

It was another week before Mother found the time to take me shopping. She had her own holiday list to take care of, so it was convenient for me to tag along. Charles came too, to help carry the parcels. Over the next few hours, I managed to find gifts for Mother, Alberta, Charles, Alice, Gary, and even Harold and Bruce. I even found the perfect scarf for Father, the softest wool in a black and beige plaid. The shop wrapped everything in white boxes and red velvet ribbons. I felt as though Christmas Day itself couldn't be jollier than that day of shopping with Mother.

As the holiday neared, I saw less and less of Father. He spent longer hours at the tobacco shop and was often home well after dark. Mother remarked once or twice that he had his own shopping to do and not to fret so, though I could tell by her worried expression that something about Father's absences troubled her.

On Christmas Eve, it was after seven by the time I heard the car engine rumbling up the driveway. I hurried to the back porch and watched as Father climbed out of the car, opened the garage door, and returned behind the wheel to park it inside. But though I waited, the engine did not cut out and the white exhaust continued to spiral out into the cold, wet night. A tickle of concern percolated deep inside my chest. Why hadn't Father turned off the engine? Why hadn't he come into the house?

I pushed through the screen door and hurried to the garage. Inside was the Lincoln, it's engine humming. I approached the driver's side door and knocked on the window.

Father, who had been staring ahead, shuddered in surprise. When he saw me, he quickly turned the key, cutting the ignition, and opened the door to exit the car.

"Polka Dot," he said, embracing me. "Where's your coat? It's bitterly cold out here."

"I was waiting for you," I told him. "What were you doing?"

Father shoved the door closed. Together we walked out of the garage, and Father pulled the garage door shut behind us.

"Just thinking," he said finally.

"Thinking about what?"

He pulled me close and rubbed my bare arms, which were now covered in goose pimples from the cold.

"Just thinking," he said.

That night I could hardly sleep. Of course, I had long since stopped believing in Santa, but I couldn't help longing to hear the tinkling of his sleigh bells. When I was little, I'd lay awake as long as I could, waiting for them. Only once they sounded would I finally fall deep asleep. It was only two years ago that Charles told me that it had been Father ringing the bells year after year. On one hand, I'd felt disappointed to discover it had all been a farce, but on the other hand, that Father would keep up the charade year after year just so I could experience the magic of Christmas made me love him all the more. But though I waited long into the night, this year, the ringing never came.

I must have fallen asleep at some point because Christmas morning dawned bright and clear. I leapt out of bed, fearful that I'd slept in too late. Flinging open my blinds, I was greeted by a world of white. Snow had fallen through the night blanketing the trees and our yard, everything the eye could see, in brilliant purity. Scurrying downstairs, the smell of ham frying in Mother's cast iron pan filled the house and made my mouth water.

"Good morning," Mother said as I spun into the kitchen. Sadie had the day off, of course, to spend with her own family. It was a rarity to witness my mother cooking a meal all on her own, cooking wasn't her greatest talent, but I knew from experience that she relished Christmas mornings.

"Got a pile of scrambled eggs on the table, and ham's coming up. Do me a favor, Dorothy Ann, and pour the orange juice."

There were three glasses already set out on the table beside a sparkling pitcher of freshly squeezed juice. I poured each glass carefully, but then quickly downed one of them. The cool liquid woke my tongue, and all my senses fired at once. I refilled the glass, hoping Mother wouldn't notice I'd already helped myself to it.

She carried over the final platter balanced high with triangles of toasted bread already buttered and set it beside the eggs. Then she stood back and nodded approvingly.

"Take your seat," said Mother, pulling out her own chair.

"I don't know why we can't just open our presents first," I said. "I'm not even hungry."

"Yes you are. Your tongue's practically lolling out of your face. And besides, we're waiting for Alberta and Chic."

"When are they coming?"

"Soon enough. Now eat your breakfast."

I scooped a pile of eggs onto my plate. "Where's Father?"

Mother pierced a slice of ham and dropped it beside my eggs. "He was up late, of course, wrapping gifts. And he was taken with coughing. Didn't fall asleep until well after midnight. He'll be along shortly though."

When Father finally did join us, I was nearly finished with my breakfast, and when Mother offered him food, he waved it away.

"Thank you, but I'm not hungry," he said. His face looked drawn, and dark circles shadowed his eyes. But when he looked at me, he smiled warmly. "No need to wait any longer. Let's get to it, shall we?"

Mother insisted on clearing the table herself so that Father and I could arrange the living room, which was aglow with colored lights

168

glimmering against the brightly wrapped packages beneath the tree. I hurriedly dropped to my knees and began examining the cards, reading off names.

A knock at the door did not deter me from my focus.

"Merry Christmas," I heard Charles exclaim, followed by Father and Alice. I sprang from my spot on the floor to hug them. Gary was bundled like a gift himself, and Alice handed him to me with a laugh.

"Would you mind stripping off this parka? He's fussing something awful, and I can't blame him."

I did as Alice asked, draping Gary's winter clothes over the back of a chair. He cheered right up and gurgled happily in my arms. Mother soon joined us, kissing Gary on both his rosy cheeks.

"Alberta should be here momentarily," she said, and as though fulfilling prophesy, there was another rap on the door. In came Alberta, her husband Harold, and little Bruce who had only had his first birthday in October. Anxious to roam, Alberta set the curious boy on the floor, and Father handed him a package with his name on it.

"Bruce might as well begin the festivities," he said. "Go ahead, little man. Open your present." Father laid on the floor propped up on an elbow and helped Bruce tear open his gift. Inside was a wooden duck on wheels complete with a lead. Harold took hold of the string and showed Bruce how to pull it so that the duck would follow, but Bruce's attention was already on the next present. He seemed particularly interested in the bows, so Father plucked one from a box and handed it to him. Bruce was immediately mesmerized, his pudgy little fingers exploring.

"He's growing so quickly," said Mother. "Soon you won't be able to keep up with him."

Alberta laughed as she took a seat on the sofa near enough to Bruce to keep him from getting into trouble. "I already can hardly keep up. The moment his feet touch the floor, he's running."

169

"He'll make a great football player," said Harold proudly.

Father watched Bruce, as deeply interested in his grandson as Bruce was interested in the bow.

"What do you think?" asked Charles. "Will Gary or Bruce make sports heroes one day?"

Father didn't answer. It was as though he didn't hear the question, like he'd been transported to another world. Charles and Harold glanced at each other, but neither repeated the question. Instead, Charles stood and clapped his hands together.

"I'll be Santa this year," he announced and began handing out gifts so that each person had one in his or her lap. Then we took turns opening them. Alice's first gift was a pink knit sweater from Mother, soft as a baby's cheeks. I received a new winter coat. Alberta's gift from Harold was a lovely gold locket with photos of Bruce inside. Everyone loved opening their gifts, but there was one gift I had intentionally hidden far back behind the tree. Once most of the gifts had been opened, I reached for the box and handed it to Father.

"It's from me," I exclaimed. "It's been so cold, and you've been so ill, I wanted you to have something to keep you warm." Father let the paper fall away and as he held the scarf in his hands, his eyes teared up. This was not what I had anticipated, to make Father cry.

"I'm sorry," I said quickly. "If you don't like it, I'll return it for something else."

"No, no," Father replied, drying his eyes. "I love it, Polka Dot. I'll wear it every day. It's just that..."

He took a deep breath and let out a tired sigh. "It's being here with everyone, our family. I look at Gary and Bruce, and it seemed like yesterday you were all that small. How quickly the years pass, don't they, Dorothy?"

Mother nodded. "Indeed, they do."

"I'm just trying to treasure this moment, keep it locked in my

170

memory like a snapshot."

"Speaking of snapshot," said Charles. "Where's that nifty camera of yours? We should take a picture or two."

Father wrapped the scarf around his neck and mouthed a thank you to me before reaching for another package under the tree and handing it to Charles.

Charles read his name aloud, a look of confusion on his face. Inside was Father's camera.

"Why—?" he began.

Father waved away the question like he had waved away breakfast. "You're young," he told Charles, "with your whole future ahead of you. Document it. Don't let a single moment like this pass into oblivion."

"Well then," said Charles, "I'll start today. Thank you, Dad."

And with Charles' instructions, we all gathered around the tree, Father standing in the middle of us all with his scarf wound proudly around his throat, and Charles snapped the shot, capturing the moment forever.

Chapter Thirty

THE DAY AFTER Christmas was Father's fifty-eighth birthday. Alberta's had been on the tenth, so we celebrated both before Alberta, Harold, and Bruce headed back to Chicago. Father seemed delighted as he made a wish and blew out his candles, and then opened his gifts. He was the happiest I'd seen him in months. But after Alberta left, his demeanor shifted into what I could only describe as gloomy.

The good news was that by January, his cough had dissipated somewhat, though sometimes he wheezed instead.

"It's these damned cigarettes," he said angrily one night, crushing a handful of them into the garbage can. It was the last time I ever saw him with a cigarette in his hand.

The cold, snow-laden weeks and months of winter crawled by. I'm ashamed to admit that I became so focused on my studies and spending time with Betty and Judy that I'd all but forgotten poor Walter—until a letter arrived from him. I found it waiting for me on the kitchen table after school one day, a plain white envelope with my name and address written across the front in his familiar scrawl. I hesitated upon seeing it, and I was stabbed by a hot feeling of shame. Our final day together came back, the laughter and the fun we'd had in sharp contrast to our silent parting.

I cautiously lifted the envelope and glanced around the kitchen. Neither Mother nor Sadie was about, though I could hear them in other rooms: Mother's feet shuffling across the carpeted floor in her bedroom, Sadie humming on the back porch, likely hanging laundry.

I opened the letter, dated two weeks before:

February 25, 1939

Dear Dottie,

I've written you a dozen times since you left, but I haven't had the courage to send them. Don't know how many times I can say it, but I'm sorry. Sorrier than you'll ever know. I crossed the line that day at Tashmoo, and I've regretted it ever since.

No. That's a lie. I'm glad I took your hand, Dottie. I'd wanted to for so long. That's the truth of it, but it wasn't right. We've been friends our whole lives. Can't we forget what happened? Can't we go back to being friends? Winter's been extra long and extra cold not hearing from you, and I'm afraid you've got a grudge against me.

Please forgive me.

Summer's coming in a few months. The fish'll be jumping into the boats pretty soon. They say last summer's festival will be an annual event from now on. I'm so looking forward to the lemonade and pie again. I hope you're coming. Please tell me you're coming. It would never be the same without you.

Your old pal,

Walter

I folded the paper and slipped it back inside its envelope, then held it in both hands against my chest for a good, long while. The backs of my eyes burned with tears as I determined to write him back, to tell him he was indeed forgiven and that I welcomed his friendship more than ever, but just then, Mother appeared in the doorway.

"You're home," she said, unsurprised. "Get to your schoolwork, and then help Sadie with supper. I've got a headache coming on."

She gave me a half-hearted smile and then returned to her room. I had my doubts about her reason for retreating. Lately, she and Father had both seemed distant and distracted, as if an invisible barrier had been erected between them and the rest of the world. I couldn't imagine why. I hadn't heard them argue, and nothing was amiss that I was aware of. Things just seemed — different.

I retired to my room and completed my assignments and then joined Sadie in the kitchen. Mother and I ate alone at the table, though I noticed Mother barely touched her soup. Sadie had gone home after setting the table, so I cleared and washed up while Mother headed to the living room to knit.

By the time Father arrived home that night, the sun had set hours earlier, and his dinner sat cold on the table. Mother had long ago abandoned her knitting and stood by the fireplace, her hands wrapped around her elbows, lines of irritation etched in her face.

I was listening to the wireless, the volume as low as it would go, when I heard Father's car pull into the driveway. We waited for the telltale sound of the garage door closing and Father coming in through the back door. Mother hesitated only a moment or two before marching into the kitchen. I could hear them through the door.

"Your dinner's cold, Bert."

"That's all right," Father replied in a tired voice. "I'm not hungry anyway."

"That's not the point. Your shop closed two hours ago. Where have you been?"

"Just about. Nothing to concern yourself with, Dorothy."

"But I do concern myself. Your daughter waits for you to come home, and sometimes she's in bed before you do. What are you doing? I've a right to know."

There was a long pause before Father replied.

"I drive. That's all. I drive around town. I just — I just need time to myself, that's all."

"I see." Mother's voice was edged with hurt, I could tell. Father continued.

"It has nothing to do with you or Dottie. I've just not been myself lately. Driving around helps clear my head."

"I see," Mother said again. "Well, I suppose I oughtn't prepare dinner for you anymore."

Another pause, the sound of a plate clinking against the tile counter. Mother must have taken Father's plate to the sink.

"I'm sorry," said Father. "I didn't intend—"

"It's no trouble," Mother cut in. "I just think as your wife, I've a right to know. You're right, you haven't been yourself lately. But I think you owe it to Dottie at least to be home at night."

"Of course. Of course. I'm sorry."

Silence came from the kitchen after that. Eventually, I heard the faucet turn on, the sound of scraping as Mother emptied Father's plate into the garbage. I turned off the wireless and tiptoed to the kitchen door, pushing it open just enough for me to see her standing at the sink washing dishes furiously. But she also sniffed and raised the heel of her dry hand to her eyes, forcing away a tear or two.

That night, I sat at my desk in my dark room with just the table lamp on. I tried to push my parents' conversation out of my head. It wasn't meant for me, and despite what Mother had said, Father owed

175

me nothing.

My fingers gripped the pen, hovering over the blank sheet of stationary. Finally, I forced myself to put pen to paper:

March 10, 1939

Dear Walter,

I apologize for waiting so long to write to you. Truthfully, I wasn't sure what to say. After what happened at Tashmoo Park, I thought you must hate me. I almost hated myself. I treasure our friendship and always will. Some of my fondest memories of Algonac include you. So of course, I am looking forward to this summer! Ours will be the best decorated boat of the parade. See you in a few months.

Dottie

Then I set the pen down, crawled into bed, and turned out the light.

Chapter Thirty-One

THE FOLLOWING FRIDAY, March 17th, school couldn't let out fast enough for me. Father had been promising to take me to see Shirley Temple's newest film as soon as it hit the screen, and today was that day.

After saying a quick goodbye to Judy and Betty, I walked home as briskly as I could. I was out of breath by the time I rushed through the front door which banged as I opened it too energetically. Mother was there waiting, feather duster in hand.

"Dorothy Ann!" she said disapprovingly.

"Hello, Mother," I replied, then planted a quick kiss on her cheek, which softened her expression somewhat.

"What's gotten into you? All flustered and red in the face."

"Nothing," I replied. "Lots of homework! Gotta get to it!"

I hurried to my room, shut the door, and dove right in, though I had a hard time focusing on my assignments, my mind was so anxious.

I was still struggling through my outline on Ancient Egyptian history when I heard Father's car turn into the drive. I hurried to my window and saw him walking toward the house ever so slowly with his shoulders hunched against the wind and cold. What if he'd forgotten about our plans?

I couldn't help myself. I tore out of my bedroom and rushed to the back door to meet Father, who came in as if he had all the time in the world.

"Polka Dot?" he asked curiously when he spotted me waiting for him in the kitchen.

"Hi Daddy."

He must have read the anticipation in my face because he withdrew the folded newspaper from beneath his arm and tapped it against his palm. He was teasing me, drawing the moment out, or so I hoped.

"What are you doing just standing there?" he asked, opening the paper and glancing at the front page. "Shouldn't you be doing your homework?"

"It's nearly done," I replied. "Are you—are we—?"

I couldn't bear to finish the question for fear that he had indeed forgotten. But finally, he reached into his breast pocket and pulled out two pieces of paper with brightly colored print. He fanned them between his fingers so I could see.

"The tickets!" I nearly shouted, but then reigned in my enthusiasm to avoid Mother's disapproval. "You remembered!"

I threw my arms around him and never wanted to let go. He felt so warm in his tweed jacket smelling of mint and tobacco.

"Seven o'clock showing," he said. "Plenty of time to finish your schoolwork and help clean up after supper."

He gave me a gentle smile but something about it was a little off, I thought. It lacked his usual luster. In fact, for several days now, ever since that night in the kitchen, I'd noticed it.

"We're having salmon tonight," I told him. "Sadie's already got it in the oven, and rice pilaf's simmering on the stove."

Father glanced at the medium-sized pot to his left. "I'm not very hungry tonight," he said. "Give Sadie my apologies. More for you though, eh?"

"I do like salmon," I said, hiding my concern. I tried to remember the last time I'd seen him eat a full meal after work. It had been weeks.

"Besides, we have to save room for popcorn, don't we?"

His smile grew a little wider, and my concerns vanished for the moment. Of course, I was just being silly. If he wasn't hungry, he wasn't hungry.

"Run along now," he said. "We'll head out right after you're done eating."

"And cleaning up, like you said. Mother will insist I help with the dishes."

"I'll lend a hand as well to move things along. Don't worry, Polka Dot. We've got plenty of time."

Getting through dinner and dishes was a new kind of torture, but finally, at 6:30pm Father and I set out for town. The Capitol Theater wasn't the only movie house in Cleveland, but it was our favorite. Built in 1921, it had started out as a silent film theater complete with a Wurlitzer organ but had since been converted for talkies. Gordan Square and Arcade, of which the theater was the highlight, occupied the corner of West and 65th Streets. From the outside it was hard to tell just how grand it was inside, but once you walked through the glass front doors, it was like stepping into an entirely new world.

Of course, the marquee was always a sight to see, especially at night, with its bright lights and bigger than life posters and lettering announcing the latest picture. But the interior was the best: row upon row of leather seats on the main floor and balcony, a screen as tall as the building itself, a chandelier, and even a guest lounge on the second floor where patrons could gather during the intermissions.

Of course, Father and I bought popcorn (no sense seeing any movie without popcorn) and found our seats. We always liked the front of the balcony, not because the seats were cheaper but because I loved looking down on the entire theater, like a Roman Goddess surveying the mortals on earth.

Father and I settled into our seats. The theater was filling fast. It was opening night, after all, and soon it was just about as full as I had ever seen it.

The Little Princess was Shirley Temple's twenty-eighth movie in only seven years. I'd seen plenty of them: *Rebecca of Sunnybrook Farm, Heidi, The Littlest Rebel,* and a few others. Looking back, those sparkling eyes and dimples brought joy to millions across the country during a very difficult period in our history. What came to be known as the Great Depression had affected everyone in one way or another. Many lost their savings, some lost jobs or businesses, others lost everything. Shirley Temple and her infectious smile, songs, and dancing gave Americans hope.

I was only four years old when the stock market crashed, and in the decade that had since passed, things had pretty much returned to normal in Cleveland. At least that's what I heard Mother say once.

"It's a relief to see things back to normal around here." She'd said it to the grocery clerk one Saturday morning while selecting tomatoes from a bin full of them.

As a child, I had never considered how or if the Depression had affected my own family. We always had hired help in the house, and my father's tobacco shop remained open through it all. But later, much later, I couldn't help but wonder if it had taken its toll on Father in ways I nor anyone else knew.

The lights dimmed, and the theater filled with applause. Then we all settled down. *The Little Princess* was everything I hoped it would be. I had read the book by Frances Hodgson Burnett, of course. The tale of the little girl whose father enrolls her in a London boarding school while he serves the British Empire as a soldier in India is a story still near and dear to my heart. When the father is presumed dead, the little girl is made to act as a servant to the school and the other students. All ends well, of course. She discovers her father isn't dead at all and they are reunited. While the movie left out some details

180

from the novel, Shirley Temple did a fine job portraying Sara Crewe and expressing both the grief of losing her father and the hope that things would get better.

It was a very satisfying movie. I would have gladly bought another ticket to see it again, but the lights came up, and everyone began exiting the theater.

Father remained in his seat, quietly staring at the now blank movie screen.

"It was a marvelous movie, wasn't it?" I asked him.

"Yes, yes it was. Of course," he replied distractedly, as if his mind were far away.

Finally, once most of the balcony was vacated, we made our way downstairs and back to our car. The streets were alive with people and sounds coming from the arcade and the restaurants nearby. I was still so energized from the movie, I thought I might ask Father if we might stop for ice cream. But when I looked at him, he seemed deep in reverie, his expression full of thought.

We made it to the car, and Father opened the passenger side door for me. Then he slid in behind the wheel, but he did not take his keys from his pocket. Instead, he placed both hands on the wheel and stared out the window where a large group of kids, some I recognized from school, were crossing the street in front of us, laughing and chatting happily. But even after they passed, Father remained still.

I turned to look at him, wondering what he was waiting for when I saw a tear roll down his cheek. He was crying.

"Daddy?" I asked, laying my hand on his arm. "Are you all right?"

He came to himself then, my voice seemingly pulling him back from wherever he'd gone in his mind. He pulled the handkerchief from his pocket and hastily wiped his eyes, then blew his nose.

"Must be the movie," he said with an unconvincing smile. "It was marvelous, just as you said."

Then Father fished out his keys and started the ignition. We drove home in silence, Father having vanished into some other world again, a world I was unable to join him in. I wondered what he was thinking about, he looked so serious, but I dared not ask. But now, so many years later, I wish I had.

Chapter Thirty-Two

MORE THAN A week had passed after the movie, after seeing Father cry. I hadn't known what to make of it, so I acted as if nothing out of the ordinary had happened. Soon I was immersed in school again and enjoying the company of Judy and Betty every day at lunch.

"What is that?" Judy asked one day when a white envelope fell out of my book bag. She snagged it up before I could retrieve it.

"Give it here," I told her. I tried to snatch it back, but she held it out of my reach.

"It's a letter," she told Betty. "A letter from—" She read the return address. "From that boy in Algonac!"

"Walter?" asked Betty with a giggle.

"Let me have that," I said trying not to overreact. "It's just a letter, big deal."

Judy gave the letter back. "We know, but you haven't mentioned him in a while. Not since you came home after vacation. I'd assumed things had cooled between you."

"There was never anything between us to cool." I took my usual seat at our favorite lunch table and removed my paper-wrapped sandwich from my book bag. Sadie had also sent the biggest, reddest apple I'd ever seen. I couldn't wait to eat it.

But Judy and Betty's eyes were wide with curiosity. After Walter's

183

letter in February, I'd finally gotten up the courage to write back. It was brief, just a paragraph on a page of the stationary he'd given me. I had said I was glad we were friends and that I looked forward to next summer too. I'd received a new letter in response but hesitated to open it. That's when Judy spied it in my notebook.

I set my sandwich down and opened the letter, first reading it silently to myself. Fortunately, he'd made no mention of what happened last summer.

"Well, what does it say?" prodded Judy.

"He says his father's looking at a new boat," I told the girls. "And my Aunt Florence has recruited him to help plan the Independence Day festival."

"What else?" asked Betty.

"He says he misses me," I added, "and looks forward to seeing me again this summer. He's got loads planned: fishing, swimming, boating. The things we've always enjoyed since we were kids."

Judy fell silent, clearly disappointed at the letter's innocuous nature. I casually tucked the plain note back into the envelope and slid it into a safe pocket in my bag. Betty started to eat her cheese sandwich.

"You are going to write him back?" she asked.

"Of course, I'll write back," I answered. "Why wouldn't I?"

The lunch bell rang, and Judy and Betty hurried off to their classes. Later that day, I sat at my desk with my pen poised over another sheet of Walter's stationery. It had been more than seven months since I'd last seen him. I should have written half a dozen letters by now, each one pages and pages long. What I'd sent not long ago had said very little and, I was certain, was not what Walter wanted or needed to hear.

I set my pen down and lay on my bed. Knickers leapt soundlessly up beside me and snuggled in close, her tail flicking. I thought again of the day Walter and I had had at Tashmoo, how he'd held my hand as we dashed, giggling, through the park. The truth was, Walter and I had held hands lots of times, but as friends, pulling each other along, urging one another to hurry or to catch up. Things had always been uncomplicated between us. But when he reached for my hand at the park that day, it felt different. His eyes, the way he looked at me, sent a delicious shiver all through me. I hadn't expected to feel that way, hadn't wanted to feel it. I couldn't admit it then, but I liked him looking at me that way. Should I be honest and tell him? If I did, where would that lead? Maybe I should simply apologize and leave it at that.

"Life can be so complicated, can't it?" I asked Knickers, who responded with a gentle purr. She nudged my hand, and I stroked her fur. Why couldn't boys be like cats? Just be satisfied with the way things were, never expecting anything more.

In the end, I decided to postpone my response to Walter's letter. I slept well Friday night and spent the bulk of Saturday helping Mother clean the house. Father called into the shop sick and spent most of the day in bed. Sunday, Mother and I went to church without him. Alice and Charles came for lunch afterwards. We kept our voices down so as not to disturb Father, or Gary, who was napping in his pram in the front room.

"Is Dad all right?" Charles asked over a slice of Sadie's pecan pie. "I haven't seen much of him lately, and when I have, he looks worn out."

"Can't shake that cold," said Mother. "I've told him to see a doctor."

"Has he?"

"I assume so, though he hasn't said anything to me about it. He keeps insisting he's fine. And you know how your father is," Mother added, spooning a dollop of whipped cream onto her plate. "He hates me interfering."

Alice gave me a sideways glance, as if I might have more answers,

185

but I didn't.

The house seemed especially quiet and empty after Alice and Charles had gone home. It rained a little but not for too long. Mother knitted in the front room, but she opted to keep the radio off. So, I retired to my room. I'd started feeling a little achy during dinner and hoped I wasn't coming down with a cold of my own. Mother would surely keep me home from school if I did, and I wanted so much to see my friends, though I could certainly do with a day off from Algebra.

As I lay on my bed with Knickers curled up beside me, there was a soft rap at my bedroom door.

"Come in?"

The door opened, and Father stepped into the room dressed in his robe and slippers. It was the first I'd seen him all day.

"Are you busy, Polka Dot?" he asked hesitantly, his hand resting on the doorknob.

"Of course not. Are you feeling any better?"

I sat up on the side of my bed while he took the chair at my desk.

"I'm fine, just fine," he said quickly as though wishing to brush away my question. Knickers jumped gracefully from the bed to Father's lap. He gave her a scratch behind her ears before she jumped to the floor and skittered away.

"I won't stay long," Father continued. "I just wanted to give you this." He held out three one dollar bills.

It wasn't often that my parents doled out money for no good reason. Father was always quick to pay me a quarter for doing chores, but three whole dollars!

"What's this for?" I asked, wondering what jobs he wanted me to do. Surely, for that much I'd be taking on more than I wanted. I at least deserved to know what I was getting into.

Father coughed into his fist, that same stubborn, wheezy cough he'd had for months now and wouldn't go away.

186

"I noticed you read *Elsie Dinsmore* again," he said, indicating my copy on the bedside table. "It's getting worn out."

"I've read it three times now," I answered proudly. "It's my favorite book."

Father adjusted his spectacles. "Well, how would you like a brand new copy? Or another book altogether?"

I was astonished. "A new book?"

"Tomorrow is Monday. I'll be at work or I'd take you myself, but I thought maybe your mother or Larry could drive you to the store after school."

He again held out the three bills. I accepted them gratefully. They couldn't have been more beautiful if they'd been gold.

Father stood up, clearly pleased that I'd accepted his gift. "And one other thing…"

He reached into his robe pocket and pulled out his lighter. His cherished engraved silver lighter. He held it out to me.

"I want you to have this," he said. "Not to use, mind you. You're a young girl, and I hope you never take to smoking. Nasty habit."

"But that's yours," I said. Giving me money was one thing, but why would he part with something that meant so much to him? "Mother gave it to you."

"Well," he said, weighing it thoughtfully in his palm, "I won't be needing it anymore. Please take it."

His words sounded urgent, so I curled my fingers around the metal, warm from his hand. I rubbed my thumb across the inscription as I had so many times before.

To Bert, with love, Dorothy

"Thank you," I said, not knowing what else to say. "I'll treasure it always."

"That's a good girl." He leaned over me and pressed his lips to my forehead, something he had done thousands of times. But tonight he lingered, his kiss lasting several seconds. Then he brushed a hand over my hair and gave me a warm, gentle smile.

"Good night, Polka Dot."

"Good night, Daddy."

He slipped out the bedroom door and closed it quietly behind him.

For years, decades, after that, I often replayed Father's visit to my room that night. I've exhumed every word, every breath, every glance of his eye trying to discover what I must have missed, some message he must have been trying to tell me. But I've since come to understand that he was beyond messages, beyond hope. His decision had been made.

That night, I fell asleep with Father's lighter clutched in the palm of my hand. It was last time I'd ever see him alive.

Chapter Thirty-Three

THE NEXT MORNING, I longed to sleep in. Though it was nearly April, the weather was still gloomy, and I could feel the damp cold seeping in through the window. Sunday had been a balmy seventy-five degrees, but Monday dawned with a thick crust of ice encasing everything. It was as if nature itself had decided to mark this day as bleak.

Despite the temptation to stay curled up under my quilt all day, I anxiously looked forward to my bookstore excursion with Alice after school.

Classes moved sluggishly, and when the final bell rang, I leapt from my seat and rushed home where I hurried through my homework as fast as I could. I admit that I didn't pay as close attention to the quality of my writing or the answers as I normally would have, I was simply too excited to focus. The three dollars Father had given me lay on my desk, summoning me to get on with it already.

It was after four by the time Alice finally arrived in Chic's '37 Ford for our trip to Macy's. I was anxiously looking out the front window for her, and when she pulled up, I shouted, "She's here, Mother!"

Mother emerged from the kitchen, her apron still on, and followed me out to the car.

"Thank you for taking Gary," said Alice, handing the babbling baby to Mother through the car window. "We won't be long. I have to swing by to pick up Charles from work by five, then we'll bring Dottie home."

"It's no problem," Mother replied. "Sadie and I are going to take him for a walk, enjoy some of this cool fresh air. We'll be back in time to serve dinner."

I slid into the passenger seat beside Alice, who was wearing a lovely pink sweater and plaid wool skirt. "You look nice," I told her as she pulled away from the curb.

"Set my hair this morning," she replied, bobbing her curls with her palm. We both giggled, and we were off.

It wasn't difficult selecting a book. I knew what I wanted, but that didn't stop me from browsing every title on the shelves while Alice picked out some new clothes for Gary in the children's department. He was growing so fast, she said, she could hardly keep up. Once Alice had paid for her items, I carried my lone volume to the counter. The loud *brang* of the register and the force of the cash drawer popping open sent a thrill through me. I handed over my money, received a few pennies in change, and headed back to the car with Alice.

A few minutes later, I was nestled with my book in the back seat of the car when Charles joined us, taking over the spot behind the steering wheel. He and Alice chatted about the events of the day while we drove home, but I was too engrossed in Chapter One to notice anything they said.

When we arrived, I almost felt disappointed. My new book would have to wait until bedtime. Mother had invited Charles and Alice to stay for dinner. So, Charles parked at the curb, leaving the driveway clear for when Father came home, and we all went inside.

"Dinner's just about ready," Sadie called from the kitchen. "But I could use a hand setting the table!"

Mother handed Alice baby Gary, who scrunched her face at the smell of him. "Time you got changed, little man," she said.

"I was just about to do that," Mother explained. "His bag's on the bed in the back room." Alice headed in that direction.

"We're just waiting on your father," Mother said to Charles, who had settled onto the sofa, and then disappeared into the dining room.

"Tell me about that book of yours," said Charles as he loosened his tie. "Alice told me this morning you about had a fit that you had to wait 'til after school for it."

The front doorbell chimed.

"Well," I said, "wouldn't you have if you had to wait all day for something you really wanted?"

Charles laughed. I stepped to the door to answer it. Usually, Mother didn't approve of me opening the door to strangers, but with Charles sitting close by I didn't think she'd mind, especially since she was busy helping Sadie.

"Yes?" I asked the young man on the front step. He was dressed in a blue postal uniform and matching cap.

"Special delivery," he said, holding out an envelope.

Special delivery was not the usual method for receiving mail. It was reserved for urgent correspondence and was hand delivered immediately upon receipt by the post office. That meant whoever sent this letter wanted it read right away.

I thanked the gentleman and closed the door.

"What is it?" asked Charles.

"It's addressed to Mother," I said, inspecting the handwriting which was as familiar to me as my own. "I think it's from Father."

Mother came into the room just then. "I heard the doorbell, but my hands were full. Did you—oh, thank you, Dorothy, for getting that."

191

I held out the envelope. Mother glanced at her name and our address on the front before raising her eyes to mine, curiosity in her expression. She said nothing as she opened it and slid out a white sheet of paper.

By now, Charles had risen from the couch and had come to stand beside Mother, waiting as she silently read the contents of the note. As she did so, I saw disbelief and doubt, then fear, cross her face. She handed the note to Charles.

"This can't be—" said Charles, his eyes scanning the words. Then he looked at Mother. "Do you think he's serious?"

"I'm not sure," Mother stammered. "He hasn't been himself lately."

"What's going on?" I asked, but no one answered me. Suddenly, I felt exiled from the conversation. It was if I had become a spirit no one could see. It was just Charles and Mother in the room.

"When did you see him last?" Charles asked. "This morning?"

"He left for work early. He's been doing that."

"Has he been home? Did he come home and leave again?"

"I don't know. I was out with the baby—"

Charles grew more insistent. "Did you argue?"

"No," said Mother. "Of course not."

"Did he say anything that would make you suspect?"

"No!" Mother's voice was trembling now. "He seemed fine last night. Just fine."

Alice appeared. "Gary was yawning so I laid him down for a while. What's happening?"

Charles yanked the tie from around his neck and tossed it onto the sofa, oblivious to his wife's question. "Where would he be?" he demanded of Mother.

Mother pressed her eyes closed, thinking hard. "Um, the club?" she suggested. "A café? A hotel maybe? If he was upset…"

Charles pulled his car keys from his pants pocket. "All right then. Alice, would you call the club to see if my dad is still there? In the meantime, I'll drive around town and see if I can spot his car. This letter couldn't have been sent more than an hour ago." He paused then, noticing the shock on all our faces. "It's all right," he said. "I'll find him."

He headed for the front door, keys jingling in his hand. Alice had already gone to the kitchen. I could hear her asking the operator to connect her to the Union Club.

"I'll go with you," I said as Charles opened the door.

"There's nothing you can do, Polka Dot," he said, laying a gentle hand on my shoulder. "Just stay here with Mother. Keep an eye on her. I'll call when I have news."

Alice came back into the room. "He's not there," she said. "Apparently, he closed the cigar shop early. He left hours ago."

The room fell silent except for the mantle clock's gentle ticking. Then Charles was gone.

"Dinner's ready!"

When Sadie came into the room, Mother's jumped, startled.

"I'm heading home now," Sadie added, then hesitated. She seemed to sense something was wrong. "Is there anything else I can help with, Mrs. Reid?"

Mother squared her shoulders and managed to smile. "No thank you, Sadie. We'll see you in the morning."

Soon the three of us Reid women were alone again. After more silence, Alice suggested we all sit down and listen to the radio, which we did, though I couldn't tell what programs we listened to. I don't think any of us were really paying much attention. I thought of the food Sadie had prepared growing cold in the kitchen, but none of us mentioned it.

My mind roamed. What did that note from Father say? Why was everyone so worried?

An hour passed. Then two. I fell asleep only to be awakened by Gary crying in the back room. Alice left to see to him, and soon all was quiet again. Occasionally, a car would drive by, its lights cutting bright beams across the wall, only to disappear, the rumble of its engine fading in the distance. Mother stiffened in her chair each time, her head tilted, anticipating the sound of Father or Charles' vehicles.

As I started to doze again, the piercing ring of the telephone shot through me, chasing away any remnants of sleep. Mother and I both leapt from our seats and hurried to the kitchen. Alice had gotten there before us and lifted the receiver from the cradle.

"Hello? Charles?"

There was a pause. Alice nodded, listening.

"Has he found Father?" I asked.

"Not yet," Alice told me. "Your brother's at the police station."

Mother pressed her lips into a worried line.

"What is he saying?" I continued.

Alice listened a bit longer, then she looked from me to Mother. "He says to check the garage."

A tense moment passed before Alice handed Mother the phone then hurried out the back door. But Mother did not raise the receiver to her ear or speak. We simply waited while my insides grew as taut as a tightrope.

And then the silence was shattered by a shrill scream coming from outside.

It was Alice.

Chapter Thirty-Four

I FOLLOWED MOTHER as she rushed outside. Even in the dark, I could see the smoke furling out of the partially opened garage door. Alice stood hunched beside it, her hands clamped tightly over her mouth.

"Alice!" I cried. "What is it? Whatever is the matter?"

But Alice stood frozen to the spot, her eyes open wide in panic. Mother hurried past her, waving away the smoke which I smelled now. Not smoke. Car exhaust.

As I put my arm around Alice, I could hear the engine of our Lincoln running inside the garage. Mother dove in through the garage door. A moment passed followed by the sound of the car door opening, and then the engine turned off.

"Bert?" Mother's voice cut through the sudden vacuum of silence. "Bert!"

A few seconds later, Mother stumbled out of the garage, coughing. "Dorothy, go to the house and ring for an ambulance."

My pulse sped up. "You found him? Is he all right?"

I tried to move toward the garage door, but Mother stopped me. "I said go inside! Hurry!"

I didn't dare question her, but as I ran into the house, I looked back to see Mother taking hold of Alice's arms. She was saying something to her, but Alice seemed shaken and frightened. But Mother looked her firmly in the eyes, and then Alice was nodding.

I watched as they drew the garage door open wide and after pulling their blouse collars over their mouths and noses, both hurried back inside.

What happened over the next few hours is a blur in my memory. I made the call. Police arrived, then an ambulance. I know because I saw them through the kitchen window. But I couldn't see the garage from there. I wanted to go back outside, but Mother had come to the door and ordered me to stay in the house, which I did. I tried to read my book but couldn't concentrate. What was happening? Where was Father? So, to keep myself distracted, I played with Gary, though eventually he fell asleep, and I was alone.

At some point, it must have been close to ten o'clock, Alice came in the house. She looked haggard, her eyes and face red with tears. Charles came in with her. I hadn't even noticed he'd returned. His expression was as serious as I'd ever seen him. I stood in the doorway between the kitchen and the back porch. Alice passed me without a word and vanished into the back bedroom where Gary was sleeping. She shut the door behind her.

"What's going on, Chic?" I asked, peering past him hoping to see Mother behind.

"Mom's gone to the hospital in the ambulance."

I was confused. *Mother* had gone to the hospital?

"Is she all right?" I asked. "All that exhaust. Did she—"

"She's fine. At least she's not physically hurt. But someone had to accompany—" His voice broke as he stifled a sob.

"What about Father? Is he going to be all right?"

Charles pinched his eyes and then slid an arm around my shoulder. "Dot, let's sit down. I need to tell you something."

We sat in the front room, and I listened intently to what my brother had to say. Father, he explained, had been found inside the

196

car with the engine running. With the garage door closed, the fumes had overwhelmed him.

"He's not all right," said Charles. "He's—he's gone."

And then Charles leaned forward, face in his hands, and wept.

Gone. Did Charles mean...dead?

"No," I protested. "No, I saw him last night. He was fine!"

Tears spilled down Charles' cheeks. "Oh, Dot."

He reached for me, but I pushed him away. Then I ran to my room and slammed the door shut behind me. But I didn't cry. I refused to cry. I just sat on the edge of my bed for hours, the weight of Charles' words like a granite boulder pressing so hard against my chest I could hardly breathe.

Later that night, Charles drove to the hospital to bring Mother home. It would be years before I learned that he had signed his name as a witness on Father's death certificate.

In the morning, Sadie arrived and prepared breakfast for me and Alice, but Mother and Charles weren't hungry. Charles had taken the day off work, but the house was still and quiet. Mother stayed in her room while Charles was on the phone off and on, talking in hushed, measured tones. No one told me to get ready for school, so I didn't. It was as if I didn't exist anymore. I was invisible. On passing me in the hall, Alice paused long enough to give me a beleaguered smile, but little else was spoken all day.

The next day, friends and family began dropping by with items of food: a pie, a tureen of vegetable soup, a loaf of bread. I did not return to school for the remainder of the week. On Thursday, Alice took me to Macy's for a black dress and shoes, and I thought of the new book I'd purchased with the three dollars Father had given me. I wished now I'd kept the money instead of spending it. I would have held them close to my heart forever. At least I had his lighter.

Friday night, Sadie made us a pot of chicken noodle soup before heading home. Alice and Charles had left hours earlier. Mother and I ate silently at the table, the chimes from the clock on the fireplace mantel marking the late hour. I noticed that Mother had barely touched her bowl, and the steam from it had long since dissipated. She looked lost in thought.

"Mother," I ventured, unsure really what to say. "Your soup's cold."

She blinked and then glanced at me briefly. "Is it? I suppose I'm not very hungry tonight."

I looked at my empty bowl and felt a bit ashamed. Mother looked at it too.

"Would you like some more?" she asked, already halfway up from the table. "Sadie made too much for just the two of us, I'm afraid."

Her words trailed off as we both considered what they implied. But then Mother took my bowl and headed for the stove. After a moment, I got up too and went to her.

"It's all right," I told her before she began ladling more soup. "I'm finished."

Mother nodded and set the bowl in the sink. "I need to let the pot cool before I put it away. And there's dishes to be done, laundry to be folded, floors to be swept—"

I laid my hand on Mother's arm. "It's nearly seven," I said. "Why don't you go to bed early? Or knit for a while?"

Mother shook her head. "Too much to do. I should have done it earlier, but I just didn't…" Her eyes grew moist. She swiped at them quickly as if hoping I wouldn't notice, but I had. "The funeral is tomorrow. People are coming."

"They won't be looking at the floors or our laundry."

I forced a smile, and Mother smiled weakly back. But then the dam broke as the woman who had always been as unwavering as a fortress collapsed into tears. Mother clutched her arms around herself, her shoulders heaving with unrestrained sobs. At first, I didn't know what to do. I'd never seen Mother cry before. Not like this. I had cried so many times as a child—scraped knees, lost toys, disappointments at school—Father had usually been the one to comfort me with a kiss or an embrace. It was Mother who was always the practical one.

"Once you're finished feeling sorry for yourself," she would say, "let's see if we can't fix the problem."

I waited as Mother cried for a minute or two. I understood how she felt, since I'd watched Sadie and Alice and Charles cry plenty over the past few days. And if truth be told, there were many times I wanted to cry too. But then I'd remember my promise to Grandma Pratt during her visit to Algonac, to be there for Mother when she needed me. And I couldn't imagine a more fitting time for that than now. So, I repelled my own sadness as best I could.

After a bit, when Mother's weeping had quieted., she took a deep breath and grabbed a dish towel.

"I think," she said, drying her face, "it's best if you and I keep this between ourselves. No sense dwelling on what we can't change."

I reached for her hand, and she took it tightly in hers.

"How about we both tackle these dishes?" I asked.

Mother nodded, pushing her sleeves up to her elbows. Then we turned our attention to the work to be done.

Chapter Thirty-Five

FATHER'S FUNERAL WAS on Saturday, April 1ˢᵗ. It was a beautiful spring day. The clouds had dissipated, and the rain had ceased. It seemed cruel that the sun had come out to warm the world when for me it felt so dark and empty.

Grandmother Reid and Marigold drove into town with Aunt Florence, and they stayed with Mother and I at the house, while Alberta, Harold, and Bruce stayed with Alice and Charles. Uncle John and Aunt Hat and the kids stayed with our neighbors. Father's other siblings came too, and even Grandma Pratt arrived and let a room at a local hotel.

The day was subdued despite the crowd of mourners, family and friends of my parents. We held a simple graveside ceremony at the Acacia Masonic cemetery with a pastor reading passages from the Bible and Aunt Ethel singing "Amazing Grace". Afterward, the Reid clan gathered at our place for lunch, which Sadie and the ladies' auxiliary from church had prepared: cold cut sandwiches, potato salad, and brownies for dessert.

While everyone milled about downstairs, I spent a good deal of the time in my room, just lying on my bed staring out the window.

As the afternoon light began to wane, there was a knock at my bedroom door.

"May I come in?" Alice asked, peeking through the door.

I nodded. My throat felt too tight to speak.

She came in and sat down beside me on the bed. "Most everyone's gone home," she said. "Grandmother Reid, Marigold, and Florence have retired to bed early. They'll be heading back to Algonac in the morning. Just Clara, Alberta, and your brother are downstairs, helping Sadie clean up. She saved you a plate, if you're hungry."

I shook my head. "I'm not hungry."

Alice let her gaze wander to the window where the sun was just beginning to set. "I won't patronize you with things you don't want to hear. I know you're hurting." She looked back at me, and I saw tears in her eyes. "I just want you to know, you're not alone."

She laid her hand over mine and smiled tenderly, and that one act unlocked the pain I'd been trying to hold at bay the past several days. I sat up and threw my arms around her, crying into her shoulder. Alice held me tight and let me weep.

"You've been so stalwart through this," she whispered. "It's about time you let it out. But it's going to be all right."

"No, it's not going to be all right," I sputtered through my tears. "How can you say that when Father's never coming back! And it's my fault!"

Alice gently pulled me away from her so she could see my face. "It's not your fault, Dottie. Don't say that."

"But it is—all of our fault. Don't you see? You, and me, and Mother, we just waited here in the house. Charles driving all around town, frantic. And Father was in the garage the whole time. If only we'd thought to look sooner, we might have saved him! Why didn't we look sooner?"

I burst into another round of sobs while Alice held me close and stroked my hair.

After a minute or two, I managed to catch my breath. Alice

handed me her handkerchief, which I used gratefully.

"We'll never know what might have happened if things had gone differently," she said in a steady voice. "We could drive ourselves crazy with doubt and blame, but I don't think that's what your Father would have wanted, do you?"

I thought about it for a moment, then shook my head. "But why did he do it?" I asked. "Why did he leave me?"

Alice folded her hands around mine. "I don't know. We may never know. But I know this. Bertram loved you, Dottie. Loved you with all his heart, and I know he wants you to be strong. Stronger than he could be. Do you understand?"

I didn't understand, and I never would. But I nodded and dried my eyes with Alice's handkerchief.

"Thank you," I said wadding the moist cloth into my fist. "I'm glad you're here, Alice."

She hugged me then said, "You know, I think it's time you stop calling me Alice." I looked at her, confused. She continued. "I want you to call me Larry."

Hearing Father's odd nickname for her struck me. His names for those he loved had always been his way of showing affection for them. For Alice to ask me to use hers felt like an honor.

"But why?" I asked.

Alice—Larry—smiled that genuinely warm smile of hers. "Well, someone has to, now don't they?"

The room had grown dim as the sun had set. Alice turned on my desk lamp, and instantly the room filled with light.

"Chic and Larry." Alice playfully tested the names on her tongue. "I always thought it sounds a little like Chicken Larry, doesn't it?"

Larry peered at me with a serious expression, and then we both burst into laughter.

Once our laughing subsided, we sat quietly for a while, both of us watching the stars appear in the evening sky. I don't know how long we remained like that, but eventually I must have fallen asleep because when I awoke the room was dark again, and I was alone in my bed. I was still dressed in the same black sweater and skirt I'd worn to the funeral, though my shoes and stockings had been removed and set neatly on the floor. My stomach grumbled, and I recalled that Sadie had set some food aside for me. I hoped she hadn't given up on me and tossed it into the garbage. But there was only one way to find out.

I left my room and crept down the hall to the kitchen where a faint light shone from the front room. Curious, I continued past the dining table to where the kitchen door stood ajar. I could hear voices, low and serious. Charles—Chic—was saying something about expenses, and Alberta was responding in agreement.

I moved closer so I could see. Mother was there with my siblings. Grandma Pratt too. Larry was missing, likely gone home to care for Gary.

I tried not to make myself known, but the kitchen door gave a tiny creak when I pushed it further open, and Clara turned her head and spied me.

"Don't be hanging about in shadows, child," she said not unkindly. "Come here. This conversation rightly should include you as well."

I looked to Mother for confirmation. She'd often said, "children should be seen but not heard," and I expected she wouldn't want someone my age joining in on an adult conversation. But her eyes were cast down, and she said nothing.

So, I came in and took a seat beside Alberta on the sofa. She immediately scooped my hand into hers and gave it a reassuring squeeze.

"As I was saying," she said, "it's not a bad place. The weather is dreamy, sunshine all year round. None of these endless snowy winters. And you'd love the beaches. Really. I'd go back in a heartbeat

203

if I could."

Mother was unusually sedate as she sat on the edge of the wingback chair, her ankles crossed and a handkerchief clutched in her hand.

"I don't know," she murmured. "I just don't know. Our house…"

Alberta leaned forward earnestly. "You said yourself, without Father's income you can't pay the mortgage."

Mother nodded, and I saw a tear creep into the corner of her eye, though she dabbed it away before it could fall.

"I'll cover next month's payment," said Clara. "And a little extra to get you started."

Mother smiled appreciatively. I hadn't considered that Father dying would cause problems with money. But of course, it would. But what was this talk about beaches and sunshine?

The clock on the mantle chimed eight. Mother cast a quick glance at it. "I'll have to find work," she said.

"Don't you worry about that," said Alberta brightly. "I've already called the Taylors, you remember the family I boarded with when I was there? I looked after their children that year. Mrs. Taylor has lots of friends in need of help, and she assured me she could find a position for you."

"Doing what? A nursemaid? Housekeeper?"

Mother had always *hired* housekeepers. Now the prospect of hiring herself out as one weighed on her. I could tell by the broken expression on her face. I couldn't bear being silent anymore. I had to know what was going on.

"What are you all talking about?" I asked, careful not to sound too nosy. "What's this about Mother taking a job? If she works, I can work too."

"You'll be going to school," said Clara, "like any young lady worth her salt should do. It's a parent's duty to support her children,

204

isn't that right, Dorothy May?"

Mother nodded without emotion.

Alberta turned to me and squeezed my hand again. "You and Mother are moving—to California."

California...

I'd always wanted to visit California, after all the postcards from Alberta and her descriptions of the palm trees and the Pacific Ocean. But suddenly my heart sank. It was clear on the other side of the country. On the far side of the world!

"We can't move," I stammered. "We've always lived in Cleveland. This is our home. What about my friends? Our family?" I felt a sense of desperation creeping up my throat. I looked to my brother who had been quiet through this entire conversation.

"Chic, you and Larry, you'll be coming too, won't you?"

Chic lowered his eyes. "No, Polka Dot. I've got a good job here. And Alice's family..." His voice trailed off.

"Will Sadie come with us?"

Mother shook her head. "I'm letting Sadie go in the morning. I can't afford her salary."

I didn't want to go to California, but I could see that this was not my decision to make. How would I tell Judy and Betty?

"When are we going?" I asked, dreading the answer.

Mother looked to Alberta and Clara, as if searching for conviction she herself did not have. Finally, Clara spoke up.

"If all goes well, if the house sells, as I believe it will, you and your mother will be ready to go by the end of June. You'll finish up your term at school first, of course."

I didn't want to say it, didn't want to hear what I dreaded to hear. But I had to know.

"What about Algonac?"

A fresh tear fell from Mother's eye. "We won't be going this year," she said in a near whisper.

205

My breath caught sharply in my chest as I felt my own tears burning the backs of my eyes. I'd spent every summer of my life in Algonac with Grandmother Reid, and Marigold, Uncle John and Aunt Hat, Auntie Florence...

And Walter.

I thought of the letter in my room, the one I hadn't yet replied to. I'd thought I'd get the chance to explain myself when I saw him again, but now that wasn't an option.

Mother sniffed. "I guess now's as good a time as any to tell you that Bert's mother has decided to sell the Algonac house."

"What?" Alberta asked in surprise.

"She told me last night," Mother continued. "Marigold's going to live with her granddaughter in Detroit. John and Hattie have invited Margaret and Florence to stay in Dearborn with them."

So, that was it then. The end of Algonac. I felt shattered by the idea that I might never see it or the St. Clair again. Tears trailed down my cheeks. Alberta quickly scooped me into an embrace and pressed her lips into my hair. "I'm sorry, Dottie. But I promise you'll love Hollywood. You really will."

But I wasn't thinking about Hollywood. I was thinking about Walter. How could I ever find the words to tell Walter?

April 2, 1939

Dear Walter,

I'm sure you heard about my father's passing from Grandmother Reid. I don't know what to say about it really except that I miss him. Our house feels hollow without him. And I can't seem to keep my mind focused on school anymore. When I try to complete my assignments, my thoughts drift back to Algonac mostly. Perhaps because that's where I last saw him truly happy and smiling. The memory I most often summon is him snapping photographs of us at the river. I have the pictures he took but it's him I remember, peering through the camera, his elbows bent out from his sides, the breeze tousling the fabric of his shirt.

I'm sorry to tell you this, Walter, but I won't be coming to Algonac this summer. Mother and I will be in California. Of course, I'll be thinking of you and Grandmother Reid, Marigold, Aunt Florence, and all the others. Alberta says we'll simply love the West Coast, but I imagine that even the ocean couldn't be as beautiful as the St. Clair.

Wishing you all the best.

Dottie

Chapter Thirty-Six

JUST AS CLARA had predicted, the house sold quickly, and Spring moved just as fast. Alberta's friends, the Taylors, had secured a small home in North Hollywood for us to rent and a position for Mother. I would be going to Hollywood High as a sophomore in the fall. Life for me was nothing more than going through the motions: going to school, coming home, doing schoolwork, going to bed. Betty and Judy did their best to include me in their conversations and plans, but I just didn't have it in me.

We celebrated Gary's first birthday on May 17th. Larry baked a cake covered in fluffy white frosting, and Gary got his very own piece which he spent more time squashing in his fists than eating. Chic used Father's camera to snap a few photographs of the day. I even saw Mother smile a few times, but none of us were as joyful as we might have been.

The school year ended with a fizzle. Judy announced that she'd be spending the summer in Florida with her grandparents, and Betty would be working as a part-time nanny for a local family. I gave each of them a big hug before leaving school.

"Be sure to write us from California," Judy implored. "I want to know about all the famous stars you run into."

"Don't get sunburned on the beach," warned Betty, though I

caught a glint of tears in her eyes. "We'll miss you."

I'd miss them too, but I couldn't bring myself to say it with the catch in my throat. As we waved goodbye to each other, I wondered if I'd ever see either of them again.

For the next few days, Mother and I packed up our belongings. We would not be taking the furniture, as the home in North Hollywood was furnished. Mother gave her china to Alberta, and most of Father's things to Chic. I packed up my clothes and books, and some of the dolls I'd had growing up. And Sadie adopted Knickers. Perhaps it was hardest saying goodbye to him.

In no time at all, our home felt barren and not ours anymore. Neither Mother nor I had the heart to return to the garage, so the Lincoln remained parked in the driveway. I know Mother would have preferred to get rid of the car as well, but the truth was we needed it to get to California. In the end, we filled the trunk and backseat with boxes and our luggage, but everything that couldn't fit stayed behind.

The day before we meant to leave, I received another letter from Walter.

Dear Dottie,

Summer's coming fast. Plans for this year's festival promises to be even bigger than the last. I plan to join in the pickerel contest and catch the biggest fish of the day. I had hoped you'd join me for the parade again. I've already purchased new streamers and a big American flag for the boat. I wish nothing more than for this summer to be like old times, but I understand why you can't come. It just won't be the same without you.

The letter continued with details about the town, plans for the next Pickerel Tournament, and his new fishing rod. I finished it and sighed. Then I sat at the desk in my now empty room, took a blank sheet of Walter's stationery, and began to write. I apologized for missing Algonac this summer, but I hoped to see him next year. Then I signed the letter and placed it in an envelope addressed to him.

It wasn't the letter I had wanted to write. What I wanted to do was to pour out my heart to him, to tell him how I didn't understand why my father would leave me that way, and that I was angry and confused. But how could I say any of that? It wasn't my place to discuss what had happened outside my family. I had to respect Mother's wishes and keep things to ourselves. We would get through this on our own.

The day arrived that we were to leave Cleveland. Charles helped load up the car with our things. A little bit later, Larry arrived with Gary to say goodbye. Her eyes were full of tears as she kissed Mother's cheek and then wrapped her arms around me in a tight embrace.

"You're going to thrive in Hollywood, I just know it," she whispered in my ear. "But if you get to feeling lonely or scared, call me, you hear?"

I promised I would, and then handed her my envelope. "Would you mind mailing this for me?"

She took hold of the envelope, spying Walter's name on the outside, and nodded.

"And give him my new address once we've sent it."

Next, I lifted little Gary, now a year old, from his pram. He tried to wriggle free as I hugged and kissed him, a lump growing deep in my chest. I had taken it for granted that I'd be around to watch the little tyke grow up, but now I'd be on the other side of the country. Would he know who I was? Would he remember how much his auntie Dot loves him? I handed him to his mom before the tears could come then watched as Mother said her goodbyes to the baby and Larry as well.

Chic was the last to say goodbye. He pinched the tears from his eyes and forced a laugh.

"I don't know why I'm crying," he said. "We'll see you soon enough. Get settled and then come back for a visit as soon you can."

"We will," Mother assured him, then gave his cheek a gentle pat.

We'd said our goodbyes to Alberta on the phone, so there was nothing left to do now but climb into the car. Mother settled herself behind the wheel and closed her eyes. For a moment, I wondered if she'd changed her mind about leaving, but then she opened her eyes and with a determined expression on her face, she started the ignition and released the parking brake.

As we pulled away from the curb, I felt compelled to turn back to look at my family standing there on the curb. I waved, and they waved back. Even little Gary shook a pudgy palm in my direction. The house where I'd spent my whole life stood in the background, its memories already fading. But in my mind, it wasn't Cleveland I was missing already. It was Algonac. Grandmother Reid, Aunt Hat, and all the others. Walter, Tashmoo Park, the St. Clair River, the boats, the 4th of July celebration—Father. I would miss it all.

I pressed my hand against the glass of the car window, a powerful longing building deep inside me.

"No sense in looking back," said Mother. "Time we turned our eyes ahead."

From the waver in her voice, I could tell leaving was just as hard for her as it was for me. But we were leaving together, and together we would face whatever our new life would bring.

Epilogue

CALIFORNIA PROVED TO be a wonderful place to live. As Clara predicted, I went to school where I made new friends, and Mother worked as a children's nursemaid to the Taylors' neighbors. We rented a home on Hartsook St. in North Hollywood for a while, then eventually moved to a comfortable home in Pasadena. Over the next few years, we made several trips back to Algonac, where Chic and Larry had moved permanently. After Gary, they had six more children, two of whom died young and are buried in Algonac. They lived there until the 1970s when Chic retired, and they moved to Las Vegas.

Father's prediction that I'd one day fall in love came true when I met Donald Ball on VJ Day in 1945. I'd just enlisted to join the Marines as a nurse when it was announced on the radio that the war had ended. Some friends and I were at a bar, and there were sailors there on leave. One of them, a redhead, grabbed me by the waist and kissed me. We were both smitten. Like I told my grandchildren years later, "I chased him 'til he caught me."

Don and I married on March 15, 1947. A year later to the day, our first daughter, Cynthia was born, followed by Corinne, Cherise, and Clifford. We raised our kids in Monrovia, California and eventually retired to Ventura.

Grandmother Reid lived until January 1944. She too is buried in Algonac alongside her husband and Chic's children. Mother passed away in 1972. I never returned to my father's gravesite in Cleveland, but I made it a point to visit Algonac as often as finances would allow and took my children there a few times. Even now, when I stand on the banks of the St. Clair and watch the sun set, it still fills me with the same awe as it did when I was young.

Walter turned eighteen in 1942 and enlisted in the Navy. We lost touch after that, and Larry told me he'd eventually married. Last I heard, he was living happily in Florida running his own boating business.

As the years moved on, memories of Walter, Judy, Betty, and others began to fade, but Father and my summers in Algonac remained as vivid as ever. Perhaps it was his dying that cemented the longing I felt for the cool blue water flowing lazily past the Reid home or the sound of the fish splashing and the wheel of the rod spinning as he let out the line.

I never understood why Father took his life. I suspect it may have been his health. Perhaps he had cancer. Maybe finances were worse than he let on after the toil of the Depression. Or he might have struggled with an inner melancholy that finally overtook him. He had written that note to Mother, which likely held the key to the mystery. But Mother and Charles were the only ones who ever read it, and they never spoke of it or of Father's death again. I rarely spoke of it either, though I did mention it once to my daughter, and later, to my granddaughter who interviewed me for an essay about my life she was writing for school. Larry and Chic never told their children or grandchildren. We simply didn't speak of such things in those days. However, I admit that for many years, I wrestled with Father's death, wondering if I'd let him down somehow, if I could have helped him, if I should have known. I cried myself to sleep more times than I could count, but always, Father's advice would come back to me: "It's best to remember the happiest of times and let the hurtful or disappointing ones go. Does no good to hold onto the past if it brings us pain."

Eventually, the pain of his loss began to ease, and I moved on with my life. I think that's what he would have wanted me to do. He did not want to burden us then and would not want to be a burden upon us now. The past is the past. It cannot be changed, only recalled.

Though my grief has diminished over the decades, Bertram Wallace Reid, my father, is still with me, beckoning me to watch the sunset with him on the banks of the St. Clair.

WRITES WIFE, THEN DIES

Club Employe's Body Found After Threat Starts Search

Bertram W. Reid, 58, employe of the Union Club, was found dead in the garage of his home at 1234 W. 115th Street last night, four hours after his wife had received a special delivery letter in which he threatened to kill himself, police said.

Police were notified when the letter arrived at 5:30 p. m., and Reid's son, Charles, began a search of downtown hotels. At 9 p. m. Charles went to Central Police Station and was asked by Patrolman Anthony F. Kalasinski whether he had looked in the garage. The son telephoned his wife, who found Reid's body seated in his automobile, with the motor still running, police said.

In addition to his wife and son, Reid is survived by two daughters. Friends said Reid had been in poor health for six months.

Thank you for reading

LAST SUMMER
IN
Algonac

We invite you to post a review on
Goodreads & Amazon.

For a free e-book, join our mailing list at:

www.SkyrocketPress.com

About the Author

LAURISA WHITE REYES is the author of the SCBWI Spark Award winning novel *THE STORYTELLERS* and the Spark Honor recipient *PETALS*. She is also the Senior Editor at Skyrocket Press and an English instructor at College of the Canyons in Southern California.

www.LaurisaWhiteReyes.com
www.SkyrocketPress.com

Read an excerpt from...

The STORYTELLERS

Written by Laurisa White Reyes

1

♦1991♦

Elena stood at the street corner, the toes of her sneakers timidly peeking out over the curb. Waves of heat rose from the asphalt, warping the air like water ripples. She took off her glasses and wiped them with a tissue. Then she put them back on.

No, it wasn't her glasses. The air really did seem to move. Elena had never seen that before, not in Idaho where October mornings were cool and crisp. But now the term 'Sunny California' made sense to her. It was as hot as a July afternoon back home.

She shifted her backpack from one shoulder to the other. Would the light ever turn red? she wondered. This neighborhood was nothing at all like Idaho, everything concrete and brick, the only patch of earth being a vacant lot squeezed in between apartment complexes. And the intersection of Fair Oaks Boulevard and Lake Avenue seemed as wide as the Grand Canyon, with cars zooming past in all directions. Elena wanted to cover her ears and run all the way back to the farm where she had spent her entire life until now, but unfortunately that was something she just could not do.

Everywhere Elena looked, there was movement. Across the street in front of a café, a man wearing an apron around his waist held up a large square of red and white checked fabric. He snapped it in the air before letting it glide down onto a round table. At a florist shop next to the café, a woman arranged bundles of roses and lilies in long, black canisters. Across the street on the opposite corner, a large man with a mustache stiffly swept the sidewalk in front of a drugstore. And there were people everywhere, men in business suits, women in high heels or sweat pants, kids with backpacks—everyone walking or jogging or even running. Elena suddenly missed Idaho more than ever.

"Off to school, are you?"

Elena started. Was someone speaking to *her*? She glanced around. On the steps of the building next door to Elena's sat an old woman with skin the darkest shade of brown Elena had ever seen. She wore a flowered bandana tied around her head, and in her hands a strand of yellow yarn twitched between two long, metal needles. Elena wondered what she was making. Mittens? A sweater? No, not in this heat, she thought.

The woman looked up from her knitting and spoke again, a little louder than before. Her accent sounded slanted and round, like people who came from the South.

"I said are you headin' off to school?"

Elena allowed herself a brief glance in the woman's direction but then quickly looked back to the street. This was the city after all, and Papi had warned her about strangers.

The light turned red and the flow of cars stopped, their engines grumbling and growling like animals pulling against invisible leashes.

Elena reached into her pants pocket and pulled out a brown plastic tube the length of her palm. She held the inhaler to her lips and pressed the button on the bottom of the canister. A cool mist filled her lungs. She felt a little better now, but the cars still snarled at her, and the street loomed in front of her like a black void that could swallow her whole.

Elena knew she should cross. She would be late to school if she didn't. There was nothing epic about it, really. She just had to take one step after another. But the longer she waited the harder it was to pry her feet from the curb.

"What'cha scared of?" said the woman. Elena felt her staring at the back of her head. "Cars don't bite, y'know. The way you just standin' there, you'd think they was a pack of alligators."

The woman *was* talking to her, but why? What could she possibly want?

Elena stiffened. She had to get to school. It was her first day, after all. As she willed herself to step off the curb, she tried to picture her farm and the way the fading daylight cast lacy shadows across the barley fields. She took a deep breath and lifted her foot.

Suddenly, the street rippled. Elena leapt back with a start. Scrunching her eyebrows, she peered curiously at the street, which swelled and sloshed like water in a bucket. Then the color of it shifted from black to a sickly shade of green.

Elena looked up at the city's squat concrete buildings with their sharp, straight edges. She watched with astonishment as her new neighborhood, section by section, began to transform—the café, the florist shop, even the apartment buildings all melted into mud, street lamps sprouted leaves and became trees, and where the cars had been appeared the ridged backs of alligators half submerged beneath the murky water.

Soon the entire city had vanished, replaced with a hot, humid swamp that smelled of earth and damp moss. Elena listened to the sound of croaking frogs and swatted at a mosquito buzzing in her ear. For a single moment, she forgot about the cars, and the city, and school, and just stared. She was too amazed at her new surroundings to be afraid. Then, curiosity getting the better of her, she dipped the toe of her left sneaker into the water.

All of a sudden, a monstrous gray gator sprang up like a giant mousetrap and snapped its tooth-filled jaws, missing her by inches. Elena threw her arms in front of her face and screamed.

The frog sounds and the mossy smell vanished, and the all too familiar stench of exhaust fumes filled her nose. Elena lowered her arms. She was back on the corner of Fair Oaks Boulevard, the woman's knitting needles clicking away.

The signal turned green, and the cars at the intersection lurched forward. Elena turned and ran as fast as she could up the front steps to her complex. Then she rushed inside, down the hall to her apartment, and slammed the door shut behind her.

More Books by Laurisa White Reyes

THE CELESTINE CHRONICLES SERIES
Book I: The Rock of Ivanore
Book II: The Last Enchanter
Book III: Seer of the Guilde

THE CRYSTAL KEEPER SERIES
Book I: Exile
Book II: Betrayal
Book III: Vengeance
Book IV: Hidden
Book V: Defiant
Book VI: Fallen

YA & CHILDREN'S FICTION
Sand and Shadow
Contact
Memorable
Petals
The Storytellers
Mickey Malloy, Wonder Boy!

NON-FICTION
8 Secrets to Successful Self-Publishing
The Kids' Guide to Writing Fiction
Teaching Kids to Write Well: Six Secrets Every Grown-Up Should Know

www.ingramcontent.com/pod-product-compliance
Lightning Source LLC
Chambersburg PA
CBHW031058020726
47495CB00007B/1942